"Please, Don't Stop Now, Linc."

She was practically begging him to make love to her but she didn't care.

A second later, his fingers were gripping her wrists and pulling her arms from around his neck. In dazed confusion, she opened her eyes and blinked at the harshness of his features.

"What is it? What did I do wrong, Linc?"

"Do I have to spell it out for you?" His mouth was grim. "Maybe I just don't like the idea of being a vacation fling—someone to brag to your friends about back in California."

JANET DAILEY

having lived in so many locales, has come to know the people of America. She has written 65 books selling more than 80 million copies and she'll be writing many more for Silhouette in the future. Her husband, Bill, is actively involved in doing all the research for Janet's books. They make their home in Branson, Missouri.

Dear Reader,

Silhouette Special Editions are an exciting new line of contemporary romances from Silhouette Books. Special Editions are written specifically for our readers who want a story with heightened romantic tension.

Special Editions have all the elements you've enjoyed in Silhouette Romances and *more*. These stories concentrate on romance in a longer, more realistic and sophisticated way, and they feature greater sensual detail.

I hope you enjoy this book and all the wonderful romances from Silhouette. We welcome any suggestions or comments and invite you to write to us at the address below.

Karen Solem
Editor-in-Chief
Silhouette Books
P.O. Box 769
New York, N. Y. 10019

JANET DAILEY
Foxfire Light

Silhouette Special Edition
Published by Silhouette Books New York
America's Publisher of Contemporary Romance

Other Silhouette Books by Janet Dailey

The Hostage Bride
The Lancaster Men
For the Love of God
Terms of Surrender
Wildcatter's Woman

 SILHOUETTE BOOKS, a Simon & Schuster Division of
GULF & WESTERN CORPORATION
1230 Avenue of the Americas, New York, N.Y. 10020

ISBN: 0-671-53536-6

First Silhouette Books printing July, 1982

10 9 8 7 6 5 4 3 2 1

Map by Tony Ferrara

SILHOUETTE, SILHOUETTE SPECIAL EDITION
and colophon are trademarks of Simon & Schuster.

America's Publisher of Contemporary Romance

Printed in the U.S.A.

Foxfire Light

Chapter One

*M*ost of the lime-green bedspread was hidden by the two suitcases lying open. Both were nearly filled with neatly folded summer clothes. The doors leading off the bedroom to the veranda were standing open to let in the cool night breeze off the California desert.

Joanna Morgan emerged from the spacious walk-in closet with more clothes destined for the suitcases. Her shoulder-length, ash-blonde hair was tied with a white silk scarf at the nape of her neck to keep it out of the way while she packed. Leggy and slim, she moved with an unconscious grace, her posture revealing her self-assurance and self-confidence. It was all completely natural to her, an in-born characteristic that did not need an artificial air of sophistication.

Preoccupied with her packing, she didn't notice the elegantly dressed woman pause outside the hall door. She was older than Joanna, but skillful makeup and the youthful style of her bleached blonde hair concealed her true age. The physical resemblance was sufficient for any on-looker to guess they were related but few suspected that Elizabeth Morgan was Joanna's mother. More often, outsiders guessed she was a young aunt.

The veneer of amiable sophistication fell away as Elizabeth surveyed the partially packed suitcases with surprise and sharpening suspicion. "Joanna, what is the meaning of this?" she demanded as she entered the room.

After sliding a brief glance at her mother, Joanna resumed her packing. There was a faint lifting of her chin to indicate her determination not to surrender to the intimidating ways of her mother.

"Uncle Reece is vacationing at his place in the Ozarks. He invited me to join him—and I've decided to accept." Her reply ended on a note of challenge.

There was a thinning of the precisely outlined carmine lips. "Why wasn't I told about this before now?"

With a pair of white slacks neatly positioned in the suitcase, Joanna turned and walked calmly to the chest of drawers. She didn't bother to immediately answer as she took out several sets of undergarments and carried them to the bed.

"In case you've forgotten, Mother, I am twenty-one. I don't exactly need your permission anymore," she stated. One shoulder was lifted in a shrug that seemed to lessen her stand of defiance. "Besides—I only decided this afternoon that I was going."

"You'll simply have to change your plans," Elizabeth Morgan announced with the airy certainty of one accustomed to having her wishes granted. "I've made arrangements for us to have lunch tomorrow with Sid Clemens. He's the head of a very prestigious advertising firm. I'm certain he can find a position for you in his agency."

Joanna stopped packing to face the woman standing at the foot of the brass bed. "I am leaving to get away from all these private job interviews you keep setting up. I haven't had a minute to call my own since I received my bachelor's degree."

With barely disguised irritation, she picked up the underclothes and began arranging them in the suitcase. Without looking, Joanna was fully aware of the affronted expression her mother was wearing. A trace of ironic humor appeared in the sudden slant of her mouth.

"We really have—'come a long way, baby,'" Joanna mockingly quoted the phrase attached to the women's lib movement. "You know there was a time when mothers paraded their daughters in front of every eligible bachelor in town. Now—we're dragged around to meet every prospective employer."

"I am only trying to help you," her mother declared stiffly.

"Well, don't," Joanna retorted sharply, then released a long breath. "I just want to get away and relax for a couple of days. There isn't any harm in that."

"But why on earth would you want to go to the Ozarks?" Elizabeth Morgan plainly showed her disapproval of the choice.

Joanna just shrugged. "It's been quite awhile since I've spent any time with Reece." She rarely referred to him as "Uncle" Reece, although he was her father's brother. She had always called him by his first name. Again, there was a half-smile when Joanna added, "And the Ozarks sound *far* away from Los Angeles." Her brown eyes cast a measuring glance at her mother. "You're just upset because Reece didn't invite you to come, too."

Her mother appeared taken aback, and more than a little flustered by the hint of an accusation that she was jealous. "I don't know what you're talking about," she protested. "Why would I be upset over that?"

Aware that her question had hit a sensitive nerve, Joanna continued with her packing, taking her time. "Daddy's been dead for almost fifteen years now. And lately, I've been getting the impression that Reece is more than just Daddy's older brother to you."

There was a wary attempt to guard her expression and hide her true feelings when Elizabeth replied, too calmly, "Over the years, Reece and I have become very good friends but if you are hinting that I want to marry him"—she paused, a little uncomfortably—"Reece has always been too much of a playboy to ever settle down." She stopped trying to explain her own attitude, diverting the topic to an explanation of his. "He isn't likely to change his spots this late in life."

But Joanna had guessed that her mother would love to be wrong. Her ego needed the excuse that it was Reece's inability to settle down that had kept him from marrying, rather than her inability to attract him to the altar.

Her mother deliberately changed the subject to revert to their original topic. "Since you insist on traveling to that hillbilly country," she began, on a faint note of contempt for Joanna's destination, "you could at least postpone your trip for a couple of days. I went to a great deal of trouble arranging our luncheon engagement with Sid Clemens tomorrow. The least you could do is keep it."

"No." Joanna closed the lid of one of the suitcases and locked it. "I've already talked to Reece and told him I have reservations on the first flight out of L.A. in the morning. I'm not changing my plans for you—or Sid Clemens."

On this issue, she could be as stubborn as her mother. She was going and she wouldn't be talked out of it.

The night air was somnolent and still, with not enough breeze to ripple the moon-shot surface of the lake. The dark sky was dusty with stars. In a nearby cove of the lake, a bullfrog sang its bass solo to the background music of *chirruping* crickets. It was a warm summer evening, the heavily wooded Ozark hills unwilling to relinquish the day's heat.

Where a hill sloped into the lake, a cabin sat in a man-made clearing, the new-fangled kind made of precut logs, modern rustic. Its covered porch faced the lake and ran the width of the cabin. A light burned inside, attracting the moths to the screened door. The soft whirr of their wings could be heard as they beat themselves against the wire mesh.

In the shadows of the porch, beyond the fall of light fanning out from the doorway, two men sat in a pair of cane-backed rockers. The run of silence between them was companionable. Yet the two men were sharply different and the differences were evident in a glance.

One was older, on one side or the other of the fifty mark. His dark hair was showing signs of graying, but his features retained the lean handsomeness of his youth, proud and strong. His eyes were dark, nearly black, lit by an unquenchable vitality. There was a worldliness about him that was not gained from this environment. His experience did not come from these hills, but outside them. Reece Morgan was the outsider, the "furriner."

The fact was reinforced by the creased finish of his khaki tan slacks and the silk-like material of his white shirt, tailored to fit his physique.

The cuffs of his shirt were precisely rolled back to reveal tanned forearms and the gold sheen of an expensive watch on his wrist. His hands were smooth, unmarked by callouses, indicating an absence of physical labor in his lifestyle. Yet, the "Ozark Mountain Country" of Missouri, raw and untamable, satisfied an inner need in Reece.

In contrast, Linc Wilder was a product of the hills, a ridgerunner as the Ozark natives called themselves. A generation younger, he was two years past thirty. His long legs were stretched in front of him, the rundown heel of a boot hooked over the arch of the other.

His faded Levis were worn smooth and soft, the material naturally molding itself to narrow hips and sinewed thighs. The plaid shirt had seen many washings. Its thinness was evident as it pulled across his wide shoulders. Clothes were not indicative of a man's status in the community. It was the quality of the man they judged, not his possessions, and his name commanded a hard-earned respect.

His long-bodied frame was relaxed in the high-backed rocker. A weather-beaten cowboy hat sat low on his forehead, shadowing his features. A ravel of smoke curled from the cigarette between his work-roughened fingers.

When he took a drag on it, the flaring glow from the cigarette cast a light on his angular features, throwing into sharp relief the hard curve of his cheekbones flattening out to the carved line of his jaw. The light briefly reflected the lustre of thick, brown hair before the hand holding the cigarette was lowered.

His brown eyes were light-colored with a dominant gold sheen. Some called them "painter's" eyes, the Ozark term for panthers or cougars. They were ever-alert, ever-alive to what went on around him, making his surface indolence deceptive.

Even now, Linc had noticed his older companion's intense interest in the thick forest of hardwoods that crowded the clearing. Without changing his relaxed position, he swung his gaze to the woods, a mixture of hickory, oak, and cedar.

A ghostly light, bluish in color, wavered in the distance at about a man's height. His glance ran back to his friend's curiously aroused expression as the corners of his mouth were pulled in, a controlled show of amusement.

"Linc, do you see that light? What is it?" Reece Morgan's voice did not contain the lazy, regional drawl of the area. Its accent came from another part of the country.

The rocker creaked as Linc pretended to look, then settled back in his chair. "Must be ghost-lights, the spirit of a lost soul wandering the woods."

"Please, none of your folklore and legends." The reply was heavy with amused patience.

"It's called by a lot of names, depending on where it's seen—graveyard lights, marsh lights. In the deep woods, it's known as foxfire." He

14

flicked his cigarette butt into the night's darkness, watching the red arc it made.

"A will o'the wisp." Reece Morgan gave it the term he was more familiar with.

"Right." Linc let his gaze wander back to the light, a phenomenon of nature. "It's caused by the decomposition of matter, giving off gases. When the conditions are right, there is an incandescent glow." The strange light appeared to move away, fading into the night and disappearing altogether.

"In all the times I've been here, I don't recall seeing it before. Is it common?" Reece asked with an intrigued frown.

"No. I've only seen it a few times myself. The first time I was just a boy and it scared the livin' daylights out of me," Linc smiled briefly at the memory. "I thought it was the ghosts of the Spanish soldiers with Cortez that were massacred by the Indians, come back to haunt the hills."

"A child's imagination is a vivid thing," Reece agreed and released a soft, contented sigh. He paused a moment as if to savor all that was around him, the sounds, the smells, the silences of the land. "I have been coming here, to this place, for the last ten years, yet I haven't tired of it. Sometimes, when my life becomes really hectic out there, it is by remembering all this that I am able to retain not only my sanity but also my perspective on what is important."

"It doesn't seem like it's been ten years," Linc mused, thoughtful for a moment.

"You have changed a great deal since that first summer we met," Reece observed and watched the dry quirk of Linc's mouth. "You were a regular hellion then. The following year, when I learned your father had died, I half-expected you to squander all the wealth and property your father had managed to accumulate in his lifetime."

"So did a lot of people," he acknowledged.

"You had to grow up fast." Reece considered that fact. "Perhaps too fast."

Only now and then did he see traces of the wild, devil-may-care youth. Responsibility at a young age had hardened the man, leaving him with a mouth less inclined to smile and a closed-in expression. Linc Wilder had become somewhat of a loner, a rogue, not without friends but with few who could appreciate the pressure associated with his responsibilities.

This was the common ground they shared, the foundation their friendship was built on. It was this insight that enabled Reece to see the restlessness that stirred beneath Linc's apparently calm surface, and had been present since Linc had arrived nearly an hour ago. He didn't know the cause for it, and nothing Linc had said enlightened him. He had been waiting for Linc to tell him, but now he decided to do a little probing.

"Have you heard from the bride and groom since they returned from their honeymoon?" Reece masked his interest in a casual question, referring to the recent marriage of Linc's baby sister, Sharon; at eighteen the youngest of the Wilder children.

"They stopped by the other evening," he admitted. "Sharon is still a giggly bride with stars in her eyes, blushing at the smallest remark." That statement led him into imparting information about the third member of the family, his younger brother, David. "David won't be coming home at all this summer. He's clerking for an attorney firm in Dallas."

"The house must seem empty." His dark gaze narrowed thoughtfully as Reece read between the lines.

After nine years of being the family breadwinner and stand-in father for his younger brother and sister, he was no longer required to fill those roles. His mother had passed away last fall; his brother was in law school; and his sister was married.

"I have some peace and quiet at last." Linc seemed to mock his own words.

"Now you are free to think of yourself," Reece reminded him. "You should find a woman, get married and raise a family before you become a crusty bachelor too set in his ways to change."

"In one breath you say I'm free, and in the next you're suggesting I should tie myself down again," Linc chided. "I notice you're still single. Why don't you get married?"

"If I could persuade a certain lady to say 'yes,' I would. But unfortunately—" There was an expressive shrug of his shoulders—"it seems the desire is all one-sided."

Linc knew the woman about whom Reece spoke. "Have you seen Rachel since you got here?" The widow, Rachel Parmelee, was in her mid-forties, proud and independent, and still attractive.

"Yes, I've seen her—and renewed my long standing invitation to dinner—and received her polite refusal." The reply was made with a faint biting edge to his voice that indicated his frustration and growing sense of hopelessness. "Is she seeing someone else? Am I trespassing?"

"I haven't heard that she's dating anyone on a regular basis. Be patient, Reece," Linc advised. "You are only here one month out of the year. It's natural for her to be wary. We ridgerunners are slow to believe the intentions of outsiders."

"Patient." There was a wealth of meaning in that single word and the raised eyebrow.

Linc had the impression that his friend's supply of patience was dwindling. He understood, but he also understood Rachel's mistrust. "If you were around all the time, it would be a different story."

"Unfortunately my business does not permit that," Reece replied with obvious regret and changed the subject. "My niece is arriving tomorrow to spend a couple of weeks with me." He paused to muse, "Joanna and I are alike in many ways. Perhaps she will find the same peace these mountains have given me."

"There's always the possibility she won't like it here. She might find it too tame after L.A.," Linc suggested.

"No." Reece shook away that thought. "She is too much like me."

"For your sake, I hope you're right." Linc gathered his feet under him to stand up. "It's getting late and I have a full day tomorrow."

"Come over tomorrow evening for dinner," Reece invited, rising too. "I want you to meet my niece."

"We'll see." Linc didn't commit himself. "I have to be over this way tomorrow afternoon to pick up the buckboard Jessie restored for me."

"Jessie Bates?" At Linc's nod, Reece laughed softly. "I think that man enjoys being a character out of the hills. I am never certain how much of what he says he really means and how much is an act put on for my benefit."

"There's no doubt he's one of a kind," Linc agreed. "I'll stop by after I leave Jessie's and let you know whether I can make it to dinner tomorrow night."

"That will be fine," Reece assured him.

"Good night." His hand lifted in a half-salute as he descended down the porch steps and walked around to the front of the cabin, facing the road.

Climbing into the four-wheel-drive pickup

parked there, he reversed it out of the driveway and onto the hard and rutted surface of a graveled road. It was narrow, twisting and winding, like nearly all the roads in the Ozark hills, especially the back roads. It was virtually without shoulders; a narrow drainage ditch separated it from the woods. Linc slowed once as an opossum scurried to escape the beam of his headlights. He slowed again where another road branched off from the one he traveled. It led to Jessie Bates's place.

Three miles further he turned into the driveway of his six hundred plus acre ranch. The yardlight was on, but no light shone from the windows of the sprawling ranch house, sitting on the crown of a bald hill overlooking the lake. Linc didn't immediately go inside, but walked around the house to stand on the patio and take in the familiar view.

Far below him and some distance away, he noticed the light shining dimly from the log cabin where Reece Morgan was staying. The cabin had once belonged to his family, as did most of the land around it. His father had built the cabin on speculation ten years ago, intending to develop and sell the lakefront property he owned. But it had turned out to be too far off the beaten path for summer tourists to want it as a vacation retreat.

In the end, his father had sold it to Reece Morgan and didn't attempt to develop the rest of the frontage. Neither had Linc since he'd taken over, although there was a market for it now.

He made a slow turn and walked to the sliding glass doors. Even as he entered the house, Linc knew he was too restless, too on edge to sleep. He went instead to the study where there was always paperwork to be done.

Chapter Two

$\mathcal{I}$t was early afternoon when Joanna Morgan's plane arrived in Springfield, Missouri. By the time she had claimed her baggage, signed all the papers to rent a car, and found where it was parked, she was almost sorry she had insisted it wasn't necessary for her uncle to pick her up at the airport.

It had sounded so simple and sensible when she'd told him her plans over the phone, especially when she'd looked at a Missouri map and seen it was roughly forty-five miles from the airport to her uncle's cabin. In Los Angeles, that was just across town.

After more than two hours in airports, waiting to leave and changing planes, plus another three hours in the air, she wasn't overjoyed by the thought her final destination was still an hour's drive away. She didn't take it too well when she discovered the little economy car she had rented didn't have air-conditioning.

She had already begun to wilt under the unrelenting heat typical of a Midwestern summer. Rolling all the car windows down gave her some relief as she traveled south on the highway. But the hot wind that blew in ruined the smoothly coiffed style of her ash-blonde hair.

The city limits of Springfield were about twenty minutes behind her when the gently rolling plateau gave way to sharply ridged hills. Her uncle had often mentioned the beauty of the Ozark Mountains, but Joanna had little time to spare to reflect on the scenery. There seemed to be more traffic than the two-lane highway could handle and she had to give her full attention to the road.

As the highway twisted up one high ridge and curved down to the next valley, Joanna found herself trapped behind a slow-moving fuel tanker truck. At twenty miles an hour, she crawled up a hill behind it, her little economy car lacking the power to accelerate past the truck in the rare narrow gaps of oncoming traffic. As soon as they reached the crest, the truck barreled down the hill trying to pick up momentum to climb the next, not giving Joanna a chance to pass. It was an exercise in utter frustration.

Between that and the baking heat of the sun,

Joanna was at the end of her patience when she reached the intersection of the state road her uncle had directed her to take. In a gesture of defiance, she thumbed her nose at the truck as she turned off.

She hadn't gone a half a mile when a farmer in a pickup truck, loaded with hogs, pulled onto the road in front of her. Again, the oncoming traffic wouldn't allow her to pass and her speed was reduced to a nerve-wracking crawl. Knotted with tension, she sat behind the wheel, her cheeks flushed with the heat, her temper seething.

Joanna wasn't sure when she first suspected that she had gone past the second turnoff. The farther she went, the more convinced she became that she had missed it. She glanced again at the directions her uncle had given her over the telephone. They sounded so straightforward and simple. How could she have possibly gotten lost?

A hundred yards ahead, there was an old service station built out of rock. A couple of old cars were parked beside the building, but it looked deserted when Joanna pulled in front of the gasoline pumps. She pushed on the horn and peered at the station, trying to see through the dusty windows. There wasn't any response to the honking of her horn but as she climbed out of the car, a man in greasy overalls ambled out of the building.

"Do ya' want reg'lar or unleaded?" he drawled and wiped his hands on an equally greasy rag.

"I don't need gas," she declared with a curt shake of her head. "I think I missed my turn—"

"You're lost, huh?" He didn't sound surprised.

Joanna bristled. "I am not lost. I only missed my turn." In her opinion, there was a definite distinction between the two.

He pushed the billed cap to the back of his head and propped his hands on his hips to shrug away the difference. "Lost or missed yore turn, you can call a cat anything you like, but it's still a cat. Where is it you are headed?"

"I was supposed to turn on Lake-road number—"

He interrupted her with a wave of his hand. "The number don't mean nothin' to me. I've been livin' here long before any of these roads had numbers on 'em. I wouldn't know one from the other. Just tell me who you want to see and I'll tell ya' how to get there."

"I'm trying to find my uncle. You probably wouldn't know him," she insisted tightly. "He owns a cabin here."

"Yore uncle gotta name?"

"Yes, he has a name, Reece Morgan," she retorted, no longer trying to contain her irritation. "If you would just tell me—"

"Is he that fella from California that bought the Wilder cabin?" His gaze narrowed as he interrupted her, studying her closely as if sizing her up. "The one I heard was sweet on the Parmelee widow?"

Joanna was taken back by his information. She didn't know who her uncle had bought the cabin from and she'd never heard of any woman named Parmelee. "He is from California," she admitted. "Los Angeles."

"Go back the way ya' come and take the second gravel road on yore left. Every time the road branches, stay to the left. Ya'll run right into it," he stated with a certainty she found difficult to question.

"How far is it?" she asked instead.

"As the crow flies, it's probably no more than four miles, but you'll have to go 'bout eleven mountain miles 'fore you get there."

As far as she was concerned, he was talking in riddles. "What is the difference between mountain miles and regular miles?" she demanded, too hot and tired to be amused by his picturesque phrases.

"A mountain mile measures the same as a regular mile. It jest takes longer to travel over it 'cause it does a lot of snakin' and twistin'." He grinned and bobbed his head. "Ya'll get the idea."

Joanna turned back to her car, muttering under her breath. "I already have."

The man had disappeared behind the building by the time Joanna drove away from the pumps and onto the road, going back the way she came. After she had made the turn onto the second gravel road on the left-hand side, she noticed the small signboard with the faded numbers of the lake road. It was no wonder she had missed it the first time.

Her car kicked up a fine, powdery dust that

drifted in through the opened windows. Joanna could feel it caking her sweat-dampened face. The only alternative was to roll up the windows. She decided she preferred the dust to the stifling heat of a closed car.

The graveled road had started out smooth enough, at least no rougher than she had expected. But within minutes after she had noticed the big ranch house sprawled on the knob of a hill, the condition of the road rapidly deteriorated. The little car bounced and bumped its way along the rough track, not wide enough to straddle the ruts.

She was forced to slow down to keep from having the teeth jolted out of her head. The trees crowded close to the road making it seem more narrow than it actually was. Their thick canopy of leaves gave shade from the sun but the thick growth also stopped the breeze and Joanna was going so slowly that the car generated little wind of its own. Her uncle had to be out of his mind to come here!

Old Jessie Bates was a wheelwright, among a handful of other things. Linc wasn't sure it was fair to call Jessie Bates "old" either. He doubted if the bony man was much past forty but everyone had called him "Old Jessie" for as long as Linc could remember. Maybe it was because the man was always spouting saws of Ozark wisdom, or maybe it was the way these Ozark hills had of aging a man before his time.

Either way, Jessie Bates was a colorful character and, like Reece, Linc suspected that the man deliberately played the part of a hillbilly. If he needed further convincing, he found it when he pulled into the yard of Jessie's cabin, a chinked log cabin, and saw Jessie hitching his pair of mules to the buckboard.

Turning off the engine, Linc climbed out of the pickup cab and walked over to where the man was hooking up the trace chains. Jessie was wearing new overalls, only they were a size too large. They made his wiry frame look scrawny—more of his costume.

"'Lo, Jessie. What do you know?" Linc stopped beside the near mule and absently slid his hand over its sleek neck.

"I don't know nothin'." The man straightened and paused for effect, a twinkle brightening his eye. "The heck of it is I didn't find that out 'til yesterday."

As he was supposed to do, Linc chuckled briefly in his throat, then questioned the man's actions. "What are you planning to do with the mules?"

"Zeb and Zeke were needin' a little exercise so I thought I'd use them to take the buckboard up to yore place," Jessie explained as if that was perfectly logical.

"There's no need. We can run it up the ramp onto the bed of my truck. It'll be quicker," Linc reasoned.

"It's too much trouble to unhitch 'em now." Jessie scratched his scraggly hair and shrugged away that logic. "You can follow me in the truck if you've a mind to."

"Then I suppose you'll want me to drive you back here." Linc eyed the man with veiled amusement.

Jessie made an exaggerated show of looking down at his feet. "I still got two legs. Reckon I can walk. Besides it's mostly all downhill. Zeke might even give in and let me ride him. Never know." He climbed into the seat of the buckboard and unwrapped the reins from around the brake handle.

Aware that he wasn't going to change Jessie's mind, Linc stepped out of the way as Jessie slapped the rumps of the mules with the flat of the reins and hollered to them. "Gee up there!"

There was the bunching of hindquarters and hooves digging in as the mules swung to the right. The buckboard groaned a brief protest before the wheels began turning. Linc waited until the team was past the pickup before he returned to it and climbed in to start the motor. It was quite a sight to travel behind the mule-drawn buckboard. If the truth were told, Linc was enjoying it just as much as Jessie.

His father had bought the old buckboard at an auction some years ago. He'd always intended to restore it but he'd always been too busy. Then he'd died and it had been left to Linc. He hadn't gotten around to it either, until this spring. There it was, rattling thirty feet ahead of him.

There was satisfaction in that, satisfaction

and just a trace of sadness. He had finished another job his father had started and not been allowed to complete. The same as he had raised his father's children; seen one of them marry and the second completing his education for a law degree—just as he'd seen to the burial of his father's wife, his mother.

The truck crept along behind the buckboard, the slow pace not requiring his undivided attention. His thoughts wandered. Linc didn't notice the buckboard had reached the fork in the road where it branched to Reece's log cabin and toward the main road. Since the intersection occurred on a relatively steep upgrade, Jessie didn't check the mules. Not expecting any traffic, he giddyuped them onto the main road.

The sudden blare of a car's horn snapped Linc out of his reverie. It was followed by a startled outcry and a thudding crunch. He braked the truck to an immediate stop and whipped out of the cab. He had enough of a view of the road to see the buckboard was halted and Jessie was setting the brake. The mules were fidgeting, on the edge of bolting, but obviously the oncoming car had taken the ditch to avoid hitting them.

Chapter Three

$\mathcal{P}$erspiration beaded her face until Joanna felt like one big, wet dishrag. On this narrow, tree-shaded road, she didn't need the sunglasses any more so she took them off and laid them on the car seat near her purse. She opened it, looking for a tissue to wipe away some of this sticky moisture.

Her groping fingers found the usual clutter of things but didn't locate the travel box of tissues. She took her eyes off the road for only a second, locating the small container of Kleenex almost immediately.

Her glance swung back to the road as she took one out. There was an instant of disbelief. Mules hitched to a wagon! It had to be a mirage. The car was almost on top of them before she accepted that it wasn't. A second after the flat of her palm hit the horn, she wrenched the wheel sharply to the right to avoid them, slamming on the brakes at the same time.

Even at the slow pace she was traveling because of the rough road, there was still enough momentum to bounce the light car out of the narrow ditch and onto the opposite bank. The spreading, gnarled branches of a cedar tree cushioned the impact before the front bumper hit its sturdy trunk.

For several seconds after the car came to a stop and the motor died, Joanna was too shocked to move. Both hands were clenching the steering wheel. As she became aware that she was unscathed, without a bump or a bruise, the blood began to rush through her system at the absolute stupidity of the man driving that team of mules onto the road without checking for oncoming traffic. She was out of the car in a flash—hot, tired, and irritable—her patience exhausted and her temper boiling.

The slamming of the car door was a small sample of her anger. Indifferent to the rattle of harness and chains, she advanced on the skinny man in baggy overalls now standing at the head of the mule team, trying to calm them. She was too blinded with anger to notice the second man on foot approaching the scene.

"You crazy old coot!" Joanna stormed at him, her hands clenched into fists at her side as she came to a stiff-legged stop in the middle of the road. "Don't you ever look where you're going?"

"Pipe down. You're scarin' ma' mules." The bony-cheeked man flashed her a hushing look and began mumbling to the edgy animals.

"*I'm* scaring *your* mules!" She couldn't believe the gall of the scrawny man. "What about the fright they gave me?"

"Are you all right, Miss?"

Joanna whirled in the direction of the second voice and glared at the tall, broad-shouldered man in the western hat. "Do I look all right?!!"

She felt the swift assessment of the tawny pair of eyes. The sensation was followed by an instant awareness of the georgette blouse sticking damply to her skin and her travel-wrinkled skirt clinging to her sticky legs. She had perspired away all her makeup and her hair looked like a rag mop, the style blown apart by the wind and plastered to her forehead and temples by perspiration. She caught a fleeting glimpse of humor in his look, then it was gone. But it was like a red flag to an already angry bull.

"I wasn't hurt but it's certainly no thanks to him!" Joanna turned again on the driver of the buckboard. "You could have got somebody killed! You could have got *me* killed! You must be crazy to pull out on the road like that! Those mules are a menace! They shouldn't be allowed on public roads!"

"Now, hold on thare." The driver turned a baleful eye on her. "Don't you go blamin' my mules. They only did what they was told. It was me at the reins and it was my fault for pullin' out. I jest didn't figure anybody'd be comin'.'"

Joanna wasn't mollified by his confession of guilt. "You should have looked! That's common sense! If I had been going any faster, I couldn't have avoided hitting you! You're just lucky I was going slow on this road—which doesn't even deserve to be called a road!" she added on an angry breath of contempt and was further irritated by the way the man kept soothing the mules. "In case you hadn't noticed, it happens to be my car that's damaged, not your damned mules!"

"And I'm right sorry about that, too," the man assured her curtly. "I'll pay to fix whatever damage's been done."

She looked at the man with the baggy overalls, faded shirt, and straggly dark hair. He didn't appear to have enough to keep body and soul together. Her uncle had mentioned that this area was the heart of the Ozarks and she'd heard about the poor people of these hills, barely able to scratch a living out of a soil that grew only rocks. However, at this point, her concern wasn't for his plight, but her own.

Uppermost in her mind was the fact that she was driving a rented car. If he didn't pay, she was liable, and he didn't appear to have two dollars to rub together.

"With what?" Without thinking, Joanna scoffed at the driver's offer to pay. "Some scrawny chickens?"

His head jerked as if she had slapped him. Joanna bit at the inside of her lips as she realized her thoughtless remark had hurt his pride. He shifted to face her more squarely and stood very tall and erect, his expression shuttered and cold.

"I'll pay in hard cash if it takes every cent I got," he retorted stiffly. "Ain't no one ever said yet that Jessie Bates don't pay his debts."

He made her feel like a complete ass, which didn't improve her disposition. "Just keep your money and forget it!" she muttered in angry self-disgust.

As Joanna turned to stalk back to her car, she was confronted by the second man, the younger one. His vital, rough-hewn features were cut on hostile lines, cold and forbidding.

"I can understand that you are upset because of the accident, Miss." His steady voice was low and cutting. "But you could show better manners than to insult a person by saying he doesn't have the money to pay, then refusing to accept his offer."

She was stung by his criticism and leapt to her own defense. "I'm upset and I'm hot and I'm tired. I've been driving on your wretched roads for more than two hours with a bunch of snails in front of me, no air-conditioning in the car, and in heat only the devil could tolerate. Without any warning, some jerk drives a team of mules out in front of me and my car winds up in a ditch. It isn't even my car! It's rented! I guess you could say I'm upset. Being lectured on manners is just about the last thing I'm in the mood for. I'm sorry I ever came here and I can hardly wait to leave!"

His mouth was tight and thin. "We'll be glad to help you on your way." There was a bite of sarcasm in his voice. He turned his hard glance to the driver. "Put some rocks behind those wheels and unhitch the team so we can pull her car out of the ditch."

Her attention was split between the actions of the two men, the driver as he placed chunks of rock behind the wheels so the buckboard couldn't roll backwards down the hill, then moved to unhitch the mule team from the wagon, and the tall, slightly arrogant stranger as he walked over to examine the rear of her car. When the driver began backing the harnessed mules up to her car, it suddenly became clear to Joanna what they were going to do.

"You aren't planning to use those mules to pull my car out of the ditch, are you?" she protested vigorously. "It's because of them that it's in the ditch!"

"It seems only right that they get it out, then, don't it?" the driver reasoned with defiant logic.

Joanna breathed in a deep, angry breath, and vented her disapproval on the other man, bending close to the ground to attach a chain to the frame of her car. "I told you that car is rented. Enough has happened to me already because of those mules! Get something sane and sensible—

like a truck, for heaven's sake! I've had it with these four-legged beasts!"

He paused to throw her a hard glance over his shoulder. "That makes two of us, Miss, because I've taken about all the sass I'm going to take from a woman," he snapped. "You have two choices: either shut up and stay out of the way so we can pull your car out of the ditch, or keep talking and we'll leave you here to get it out by yourself. Now, which is it to be?"

She wished she knew whether it was a short walk to her uncle's cabin or not. She'd love to tell them she didn't need their help. But she suspected it was another three or four miles—not easy, flat miles—but three or four rough and winding mountain miles. Joanna pressed her lips tightly together in a mute reply to his question, indicating with her silence the choice she made.

There wasn't any change in his expression as he turned to complete his task, not uttering a word. When the mules were hooked up to the car, he slid behind the steering wheel to assist by guiding the car. Joanna stayed well out of the way, flinching when the mules threw their weight against the car and she heard the first crunch of the tires.

The slow, steady pull of the mules began to drag the car out of the ditch without inflicting any damage on the muffler, tailpipe, or undercarriage. The combination of hundred degree temperatures, high humidity, and the air's stillness made her conscious again of the oppressive heat. She felt the uncomfortable trickle of perspiration down her neck and into the valley formed by her breasts. A cool shower sounded like heaven at the moment.

"Whoa up thare!"

Her car was sitting squarely on the road once more. Joanna walked toward it as the man stepped out of the driver's side. He was examining the front of the car when she reached it. The man in the baggy overalls was behind the car, unhooking his mules.

"Some scratches from the cedar branches on the left fender and the dent in the bumper seem to be the extent of the damages," the man announced to her.

Joanna inspected the fenders, hood, and grill for herself and arrived at the same conclusion. Not even a headlamp had been broken.

"It's a small miracle," she retorted and felt the hard pressure of his gaze on her. She lifted her gaze coolly to his face. "I suppose I should thank you for getting my car out of the ditch."

"I suppose you should," he agreed, and the uncompromising set of his features set her teeth on edge.

"Thank you." The phrase was neither sincere, warm, nor grateful.

There wasn't any satisfaction in the way his mouth tightened at her rudeness. She felt boorish and he was the one who was the country bumpkin.

He took a step to the side, out of her way.

"You'd better start the motor to make sure it runs."

A little irritated that she hadn't thought of that, she swept past him to climb behind the wheel. The motor kicked over on the first try and ran smoothly.

"It works," Joanna stated the obvious as the insufferable cowboy walked to the driver's door she'd left standing open. He pushed it shut for her, as though silently sending Joanna on her way. "Excuse me." Out of sheer stubbornness, she summoned him back. "My uncle has rented a cabin down this road somewhere—Reece Morgan. Would you tell me how much farther it is?"

His eyes narrowed into burnished slits. "No."

Her temper flared at his blatant refusal. She shifted the car into gear and he stepped out of the way just as she pushed her foot down on the accelerator. A glance in the rear view mirror saw him encapsulated in the dust cloud swept up by her car.

Very little of the dust actually reached Linc, but he narrowed his eyes against it to watch the car disappear around the next curve. He'd expected Reece's niece to be something better than that ill-tempered spitfire. Reece was so mannerly and courteous, but the same certainly couldn't be said for his niece. Linc was glad he hadn't gotten around to accepting that dinner invitation. This was one he was definitely going to turn down.

He turned to the buckboard and saw Jessie eyeing him with a knowing look. "T'wasn't polite *not* to tell her how far it was to the cabin."

"I give as I get," Linc reasoned, but indifferently.

"Morgan's niece, huh?" Jessie stayed with the subject of the girl.

"That's what she said." Linc changed it. "This time I'll drive ahead of you with the truck so you don't run any more cars off the road."

"Don't slow me down," Jessie advised as he hooked the last trace. "Else these mules will run right up your backside."

Linc didn't bother to respond to that boast, turning to walk to his truck.

It turned out to be closer to five miles. Joanna was just beginning to think the cowboy hadn't told her how far she had to go because she was on the wrong road. She was about ready to make up her mind to turn around when she saw the cabin.

"If this isn't Reece's cabin, it will be the last straw," she muttered to herself and turned the car into the short driveway. There was some consolation that the cabin looked civilized.

Before she was fully out of the car, a cabin door opened and her uncle appeared. "Joanna!" He greeted her with a broad smile of welcome. "I was beginning to worry about you. Didn't you say your plane was scheduled to arrive before two this afternoon?" As he came down the steps, he glanced at his watch. "It is nearly five. Was it delayed?"

"No," she swiftly corrected herself. "It was a few minutes late." He looked so cool and unruffled that she couldn't help wondering how he managed it in this heat.

"Then what took you so long to get here?" he frowned, then asked, "Did you have trouble finding the place?"

"Trouble is an understatement," she replied with an edge of remembered anger in her voice. "I do hope that cabin has indoor plumbing . . . and air-conditioning!" she added on a hopeful note.

"You are hot and tired after the trip," he realized. "Come inside and have a cool drink, then you can tell me all about your trouble." He curved his arm affectionately around her shoulders as he guided her to the cabin door. "And we do have indoor plumbing, but no air-conditioning. However, there is a cool breeze coming in from the lake."

"Do you mean they do have breezes in the Ozarks?" she murmured sardonically. "I was beginning to wonder."

The interior of the cabin seemed dark and cool after the brilliance of the afternoon that not even the shade of the trees had alleviated. She exhaled a relieved sigh, suddenly too tired and travel-worn to take in the furnishings of the rooms her uncle guided her through.

He led her straight through the cabin to a

screen door that opened onto a wide porch. Joanna collapsed into a cane-backed rocker while her uncle poured a glass of iced tea from a perspiring pitcher.

She took a long swallow from the glass he gave her and leaned her head against the chair back. "I swear if this hadn't been your cabin, Reece"—Joanna paused to shake her head—"I would have turned around and gone back to California." She sat up. "I left the suitcases in the car."

"We can get them later," he assured her.

Joanna settled back into the chair. "I just don't understand what you see in this godforsaken place," she sighed, remembering all she had gone through to get here.

"Godforsaken?" He frowned narrowly at her choice of adjectives. "It is far from 'godforsaken,' Joanna. Just look at the beauty around you," he demanded.

It was rare for those dark eyes to look at her with disapproval. It wasn't a comfortable feeling. His scolding tone forced her to look beyond the porch. The rocky clearing sloped down to the shimmering waters of a lake, the source of the breeze cooling her skin.

On the opposite shore, there was another ridge of mountains, cloaked in a myriad of green shades and contrasted by a milk-blue sky. A flash of scarlet in the trees near the cabin caught her eye. She turned to see a black-beaked cardinal flitting among the tree limbs. A squirrel chattered angrily at the bird's intrusion.

"Godforsaken was perhaps the wrong word," Joanna conceded, because there was the rustic beauty of nature around her, relatively untouched by civilization and untamed. "But you have to admit it's far from anywhere—and next to impossible to reach."

"That is a part of its charm," he smiled and settled into the matching rocking chair next to hers. "Its isolation. Its distance from large metropolitan centers. Getting here isn't easy but once you are here—" He lifted his shoulders to indicate how little the hardships mattered.

"You can say that but I'll bet you didn't drive twenty miles behind a fuel truck, then get stuck behind some farmer poking along to market, miss the turn to this road—which by any sane person's standards doesn't deserve to called a road." She paused to cast a wary glance at her uncle. "I suppose that *road* is the only way out of this place."

"It is," he admitted. "The spring rains eroded it badly. It is worse this year than it has ever been." Then Reece Morgan picked up on what she had said. "You got lost."

"As far as I'm concerned, I wasn't really lost. I just missed the turn. Of course, the man at the gas station who gave me directions felt that was a moot point," Joanna inserted dryly. "Then when I did find the road, I almost ran into a pair of mules pulling a wagon. I ended up going into the ditch."

"You weren't hurt, were you?" He studied her more closely, leaning forward with concern.

"No. I didn't get a scratch or a bruise. Luckily." She was able to smile about it now as she took another drink of cold tea, her sense of humor slowly returning. "I thought I was seeing things when the mules and wagon suddenly pulled onto the road ahead of me," she laughed briefly. "I want you to know that's quite a shock for this California girl."

"I can imagine." He chuckled with her. "It must have been Jessie Bates. He's a marvelous character that lives in an old cabin up the road."

"Character is right, if it's the same man."

"He was thin with overalls a size too big and hair that had probably never seen a comb," her uncle described the man who had been driving the mules.

"That's him," she nodded.

"You should hear some of the stories he tells about these hills," he said. "He is a natural storyteller. His tales are colored with regional phrases. He plays the fiddle, too, and the dulcimer, banjo. An extremely talented man. I'm convinced he dresses and acts the way he does to draw attention to himself—the way an actor would. But you'll find that out for yourself."

"I doubt it," Joanna grimaced. "After I landed in the ditch, I got a little upset and lost my temper. He took offense at some things I said."

"What did you say?" He eyed her, well aware that she occasionally lost control of her tongue.

"After he admitted that he was at fault, he offered to pay for any damages to the car. To look at him, a person would think he didn't have a dime to his name. I said as much." She was still irritated with herself for talking without thinking about what she was saying. "I hurt his pride. So, I very much doubt that he'll be interested in seeing me again." Joanna shrugged, trying to pretend it didn't matter, but she wasn't normally unkind to people—not deliberately. "Of course, I won't be here that long so there isn't much chance of running into him again." She winced. "That was a bad pun."

"I was hoping to persuade you to spend the rest of my month here," Reece stated. "I have some work that, unfortunately, can't wait until I get back. I thought it would be good practice for you to stay and help me with it."

"I don't know." Joanna hesitated. "Mother is expecting me back the day after tomorrow."

"You are twenty-one. You don't need her permission." He dismissed that excuse. "Besides, I want to correct your impression of these Ozark Mountains and the people." Inside the cabin, a telephone rang. "Excuse me." He rose from his chair and entered the cabin to answer it.

Joanna took another drink from her iced tea and leaned back in her chair to close her eyes and dream about the shower she was going to take just as soon as she got some energy.

He answered the phone on the fourth ring. "Reece Morgan speaking," he identified himself.

"Reece, this is Linc," came the reply.

"Linc, I'm glad you called. My niece just arrived a few minutes ago. Will you be able to come to dinner tonight?" Linc Wilder had become a good friend, someone Reece took special interest in, as he did in his niece.

He was looking forward to Linc and Joanna meeting. Naturally, since he had affection for both of them, he expected them to like each other. Beyond that, he didn't plan. If anything developed, it would happen on its own. But it was a wish he subconsciously made.

There was a pause that seemed heavy. It drew the jet-dark brows together as Reece tried to guess at the reason. Linc wasn't usually a taciturn man.

"Sorry, I won't be able to make it this time." Linc's voice sounded casual, natural. Reece briefly shook his head, deciding he had imagined it. "I'll have to take a raincheck."

"You are always welcome here, Linc. If you're not busy, stop by tomorrow night—if not for dinner, then later in the evening," Reece invited.

"I'll see," was all Linc would promise. "Thanks for the invitation."

A few seconds later, Reece hung up the telephone. Perhaps it was just as well Linc didn't come tonight. Joanna was tired after traveling all day. She would probably welcome a quiet evening. He returned to the porch where his niece was relaxing. She lazily opened her eyes to look at him.

"Business?" she asked.

"No, social," he replied. "I had invited Linc Wilder for dinner this evening. I bought this cabin from the Wilders. They own most of the land around it. He just called to say he couldn't make it."

"It's probably just as well," Joanna declared wryly. "I probably would have stuck my foot in my mouth again and said something embarrassing."

"I wouldn't worry about what happened this afternoon." He moved toward the door. "I'll bring your luggage in so you can shower and clean up before dinner."

"Thanks," she said. "I'm not sure I can move."

Chapter Four

$\mathcal{A}$ morning sun had already burned away the swirling layers of mist from the lake's surface when a woodpecker flew to an oak tree growing close to the cabin. It hammered at the bark and the sound carried through the wire mesh of the opened bedroom window. Joanna stirred beneath the lightweight coverlet at the prodding noise.

As it persisted, she dragged open her sleep-heavy eyelids, becoming aware of the daylight pouring through the window. Initially, she was disoriented by the strangeness of the room until she remembered where she was.

With a yawn, she folded back the covers and slid out of bed. Her cotton robe was lying on a chair. She slipped into it before leaving the loft bedroom for the second floor bath.

Fifteen minutes later, with the sleep washed from her face and her teeth brushed, Joanna descended the rustic log staircase. Her uncle was seated at the breakfast table by the window that looked out over the lake. He turned in his chair when she entered the spacious kitchen.

"Good morning," he greeted her with a brightness that Joanna doubted she could match. "Did you sleep well?"

"Ask me that question after I've had my orange juice and coffee." Her smile showed traces of tiredness as she walked to the refrigerator to help herself to the container of orange juice inside.

"What would you like for breakfast this morning?"

"Nothing." She carried the glass of orange juice to the table and pulled out a chair opposite him. "I'm not hungry when I first get up in the morning," Joanna explained. Reece poured a cup of coffee for her from the insulated pot on the table. "Thanks. What's on the agenda today?"

"I thought we could drive to the post office in Branson after you've had a chance to enjoy your morning coffee and dress." There was a brief flash of white as he smiled. "I will drive so you can enjoy the scenery and not worry about running into any mules."

Joanna smiled with a wry pull of her mouth.

There continued to be a nagging regret that she hadn't seen the inherent amusement in yesterday's incident at the time. She wasn't very proud of the way she had reacted—regardless of the causes for her ill-humor. It wasn't any justification for the way she had behaved.

An hour later, Joanna was riding over the narrow lake road again, this time in the plush comfort of her uncle's Chrysler New Yorker, its shocks absorbing the roughness of the lane. It didn't seem to take them any time to reach the place where she'd had her accident.

"There should be a sign posted that says Mule Crossing," she suggested, pointing out the spot to her uncle as they approached it.

He smiled in acknowledgment of her joking remark. "Jessie Bates has his cabin just down the road," he explained.

"Does he have a family?" she asked, suddenly wondering if the tall cowboy had been his son, even though there wasn't any resemblance.

It occurred to her that she hadn't mentioned the presence of a second man to her uncle, but it hardly seemed important now. Remembering the censure that had been in the man's hard, golden-brown eyes stirred some of the previous day's antagonism to life.

It didn't matter that her behavior had warranted his criticism. Since her resentment of the cowboy was at odds with her regret, that was an additional reason not to mention to her uncle the presence of a third party at the accident.

"No. To my knowledge, Jess has never been married," Reece replied to her question as they passed the spot where her car had gone into the ditch without slowing.

Settling back in the richly upholstered car seat, she mused aloud, "I suppose there are a lot of hillbillies around here." She wasn't conscious that there had been anything derogatory in her use of the word.

"I don't doubt that there are many, but don't make the mistake of believing that simply because they live in the *backwoods* that they are *backwards*." He stressed the two words to be certain she was forming an incorrect perception of Ozark natives. "In their own way, these natives are extremely worldly—as intelligent and shrewd as any corporate executive."

"I won't make the mistake," Joanna promised with a smile.

After covering a few more miles of the lake road, a white board fence ran parallel with them. Cattle grazed in the grassy tree-studded meadow it enclosed. Joanna noticed again the ranch house sitting back from the road on the mountain knoll.

"That's a beautiful home," she remarked to her uncle. "Who lives there?"

"Linc Wilder." His sideways glance was slightly mocking. "He happens to be fourth generation hillbilly." And Joanna knew this was an example to prove his statement that hillbillies were not backward. "Very few describe themselves as hillbillies," he explained. "They use the term ridgerunner. I'm sure you must have noticed that most of the roads here run along the mountain ridges, hence the name."

As they turned onto the main road, Joanna gazed out the window at this ancient mountain country. Since she wasn't driving, she could ignore the traffic and admire the scenery instead.

From the higher elevations of the winding road, she could see the rippling effect as the land spilled away in wave after wave of tree-covered mountain ridges and the diamond glitter of the lake in the nearby valley. She was beginning to revise her opinion about the wild land—and the people who lived here. She was almost sorry when the buildings of town came into view.

It was mid-morning but the day was already beginning to feel hot when they reached the resort town of Branson.

"Have you been awake long enough to be hungry?" he asked. "We can stop at a local cafe if you feel like eating.'"

"Thanks, but I'm not really hungry. I'll wait until lunch."

"Do you remember that Kewpie doll I gave you six years ago?" Reece waited for the traffic to pass before turning onto the street.

"Yes. As a matter of fact, I still have it." She

had been sixteen at the time and crushed that her uncle had brought her a doll when she was trying to be so grown up. Then Joanna remembered vaguely, "You had just come back from vacationing here, hadn't you? Is this where you bought the doll?"

"Yes, from a quaint little shop down the street. We'll stop there and you can look around. I'm sure you don't remember, since it was long before your time, but Kewpie dolls were very popular in the forties. Rose O'Neil, the woman who created the original Kewpie doll, was from this area."

"I have the feeling there is a great deal to learn about the Ozarks and its people," Joanna stated and sent him a twinkling glance. "And I also have the feeling that you are planning to teach me about it."

Her uncle neither confirmed nor denied her suspicion. "I think you will grow to appreciate and enjoy the culture of this region as much as I do." He parked the car in the lot next to the doll shop.

The picturesque building looked as though it had been converted from a two-story home for commercial use. Its stucco exterior was painted baby pink and an assortment of dolls crowded the displays at its curtained windows. It looked enchanted rather than out of step with its surroundings.

As the nearly full parking lot had indicated, there were plenty of shoppers inside when Joanna entered the doll store with her uncle.

She was drawn first to the artfully arranged shelves of Kewpie dolls for sale. The mischievous-looking cupids came in a variety of sizes and poses, bright-eyed imps that had timeless appeal.

Wandering further into the shop, Joanna realized that nearly every kind of doll imaginable was there—rag dolls, corn-shuck dolls, china dolls. They were all represented. It was a little girl's dream world, and an adult's fantasy of toyland.

Absorbed by the collection of dolls, she wasn't aware she had become separated from her uncle until she noticed him standing at a counter ahead of her. He was just greeting one of the store clerks, an attractive and mature woman with light brown hair. The woman's slimness and her erect carriage gave the impression of height although she wasn't as tall as Reece. Her uncle turned, his gaze quickly locating her.

"Joanna, come here," he summoned her with a smile and a motioning wave of his hand. "I'd like you to meet the proprietor of this shop."

The information renewed Joanna's interest in the woman, since she was so impressed with the quality of the shop. Age had begun to etch the lines of maturity about the woman's mouth and blue eyes, but not unattractively. Her smile was warm, yet polite, friendly yet with a trace of reserve. Joanna liked the air of quiet dignity the woman possessed.

"This is my niece, Joanna Morgan." Reece

introduced her first to the woman. "Joanna, I'd like you to meet Mrs. Rachel Parmelee."

"Welcome to the Ozarks, Miss Morgan." The hand she extended to Joanna was slim and smooth.

"Thank you." She smiled, liking the woman immediately. "I know you have probably heard it before but you have a lovely shop, Mrs. Parmelee." Where had she heard that name before? It sounded so familiar to her.

"You're very kind." The woman returned the smile, then inquired, "Is this your first visit to our area?"

"Yes," Joanna admitted.

"Joanna only arrived yesterday," her uncle elaborated on her answer. "I'm afraid her first impression of the Ozarks wasn't very favorable. Now I have the task of correcting it."

"I hope you enjoy your stay," Rachel Parmelee murmured.

Something had happened to change the woman's attitude. Joanna could sense it. There was a coolness in her voice and her expression that hadn't been there before. She was puzzled by it because it seemed to have happened when Reece joined the conversation, and he had said nothing offensive, nothing remotely personal that could have been misinterpreted. She glanced at her uncle and realized that he had noticed it, too. His expression had altered, a certain stiffness entering it that wasn't natural for him.

"We are keeping you from your customers." His remark appeared to offer an excuse for her sudden coolness toward them. "We won't take any more of your time."

There was a disturbing darkness to his gaze, an intensity that could almost be measured. Joanna watched the woman drop her glance to avoid it.

She took her lead from Reece. "It was a pleasure meeting you, Mrs. Parmelee."

The instant she said the woman's name a second time, she recalled where she had first heard it. The man at the service station had mentioned it. What was it he had said? Something about her uncle being sweet on the Widow Parmelee, she remembered. With new eyes, she studied her uncle and the woman.

"Have a good day." Rachel included both of them in the comment.

"Perhaps we'll see each other again soon," her uncle said. It was almost a question but it received no answer as the woman smiled politely and moved along the counter to a customer looking at a selection of dolls in a glass case.

Reece turned to Joanna. "Did you wish to look around a little longer?" he inquired.

"Another time, perhaps," she said, because she guessed that he wanted to leave.

"Yes, another time." The phrase seemed to hold another meaning for him as his glance strayed to Rachel Parmelee with a certain wistfulness.

As they exited the store and started toward the car parked in the lot, Joanna murmured, loud enough for her uncle to hear, "So that is the Widow Parmelee."

Her sidelong glance caught his startled look. "What do you know about her?" He recovered quickly and sounded only mildly curious.

"Do you remember I told you that I stopped at a gas station yesterday to ask directions?" she said.

"Yes," he nodded slowly, not following what that had to do with Mrs. Parmelee.

"When I told him that I was trying to reach the cabin owned by my uncle, Reece Morgan, he knew you right away," Joanna explained. "He asked if it was the same Morgan who was sweet on the Widow Parmelee. Are you the same Morgan?" she asked, already guessing the answer after what she had witnessed inside.

Her question appeared to make him vaguely uncomfortable. Faint lines creased his forehead. "Yes, I suppose I am that man."

"And is the Widow Parmelee sweet on you?" she prompted.

A heavy sigh came from him as he stopped beside the car's passenger door to open it for her. "I don't know. Sometimes I think she finds me attractive. Yet every time I ask her to have dinner with me, I get the cold shoulder. Linc advises me to be patient. I'm an outsider. So—" There was an expressive lift of his shoulders. "I am patient."

"Personally, I think she needs her head examined for not snapping you up," Joanna declared.

"Now, do you see why I want you to spend the rest of the month here?" he laughed at her strident defense of his attractiveness. "It's your moral support I require."

Chapter Five

Outside the cabin, the shadows were lengthening as sundown approached. Joanna wiped the last of the cooking pans dry and stacked it in a lower cupboard with the rest of the pots and pans. Folding the damp dishtowel, she neatly hung it on a wallrack to dry.

"We're all finished." Joanna turned to her uncle and halted briefly to study the picture he made, so maturely handsome and well-dressed, except for the plain white apron around his waist to protect his dark slacks. It struck an incongruous note. "I wish I had a picture of you in that apron." A bemused smile deepened the corners of her mouth.

"Why?" His out-reaching glance was curious as he untied the bow in back to take it off.

"Somehow you just don't seem the domestic type to me," she shrugged.

"Just what is the domestic type?" Reece challenged with an amused look.

Joanna was without an answer to that. She was saved from a reply by the sound of a vehicle turning into the cabin's drive. "I think you have company," she said to her uncle.

"Perhaps it is Linc. I have been wanting you to meet him," he stated as he moved past her into the living room.

Joanna was slow to follow him, taking time to hang up the apron he'd left on the countertop. The vehicle's motor had already stopped and a door had been slammed when she started for the living room. She heard the creaking hinges of the screen door as her uncle opened it to admit the visitor.

"Linc. I'm so glad you came by." The delight was evident in her uncle's greeting.

"Hello, Reece. How have you been?" There was the heavy thud of footsteps ascending the steps of the front entrance.

But it was the familiar sound of the man's voice that caused Joanna to falter in her stride a foot short of the opening to the living room. It couldn't be the cowboy. From the little Reece had told her about Linc Wilder, she had gained the impression that he and her uncle were the same age, contemporaries.

"Fine. Come in. Come in." Her uncle's voice urged the man into the house.

Joanna continued into the living room, less

certainly than before. Alarm bells went off in her head when she recognized the tall, broad shouldered man crossing the threshold. Instead of the faded Levis and workshirt, he was wearing a white shirt with pearl snaps and slim-fitting, western cut slacks of tan drill.

It wasn't his casual attire that held her attention, but the rugged planes of his tanned features—sun-hardened and strong. The brim of his cowboy hat shadowed his eyes but Joanna had no difficulty remembering the hard amber flecks in the light brown irises that glittered their message of caution.

She watched the straight, firm line of his mouth curve in a smile that gentled the hard contours of his face as he shook hands with her uncle. It was an expression that didn't last long, fading when his glance traveled beyond her uncle to notice her.

"Joanna, come meet Linc Wilder." Her uncle seemed oblivious to the subtle undercurrents impregnating the air as he invited her to come forward.

With a stiffness to her carriage, she started across the room. All her nerve ends were tingling under the study of those eyes. She knew her appearance was a definite improvement on the way she had looked the first time he'd seen her. The smooth style of her ash-blonde hair flattered her features, features that were enhanced by the light application of makeup—a hint of mascara to darken her lashes, a touch of green shadow to bring out the warm brown of her eyes, and a lingering trace of brown-rose gloss to define the curve of her lips.

There was no artificial cause for the color in her cheeks as his re-assessing gaze traveled the length of her body, taking note of the slim-fitting designer jeans that hugged her hips, and of the clinging fabric of her red knit top that outlined the swell of her young breasts.

There was a definite shimmer of defiance in her eyes when she met his glance. All her defenses were raised against him. Joanna didn't fully understand this inner need to protect herself from him. It seemed purely instinctive, a reaction beyond her control. When she stopped beside her uncle, she was rigid with tension.

"Linc, I want you to meet my niece, Joanna Morgan," her uncle finished the introduction.

The strong mouth slanted its line but it never made the full transition into a smile. His glance locked with hers, his heavy with irony.

"Your niece and I have already met, although we didn't bother to introduce ourselves at the time." He held out his hand to her, the gesture in the way of a challenge.

Joanna longed to ignore it but it would have meant a gross display of bad manners to a guest of her uncle's. She forced herself to shake his hand. His grip seemed to swallow her, the contact sending tingles up her arm.

"You have met?" Her uncle reacted to Linc Wilder's statement, the frowning arch of a dark brow directing a silent query to Joanna for confirmation.

"Yes, we have," she admitted and withdrew her hand from his grasp the instant he relaxed it. She faked an air of innocent oversight when she met her uncle's puzzled glance. "Didn't I mention that there was another man present yesterday when my car landed in the ditch?"

"No, I don't recall that you did," Reece frowned in an effort to remember what she had said.

"I must have forgotten." She made light of the omission with a dismissing shrug.

Reece accepted her explanation that it had been an oversight and moved away from the door, inviting them to follow by his action. "Joanna told me about the incident on the road yesterday," he admitted to Linc.

"Did she?" The mocking lilt of his voice dryly intimated that Joanna had colored the story so she wouldn't be seen in a bad light.

Her retort was quick. "Yes, I did. Reece knows me very well—and my embarrassing habit of saying the wrong thing at the wrong time."

"Yes, Joanna felt badly about some of the things she said to Jessie." Her uncle corroborated her assertion that she had been candid about her role in the events that transpired after her car landed in the ditch. Reece paused near the chintz-covered sofa positioned in front of the brick fireplace. "May I bring you some coffee, Linc?"

"Please," he accepted.

"I'll get it," Joanna volunteered, welcoming an excuse to leave the room.

"No." Her uncle firmly rejected the offer. "You stay here. I want you and Linc to get acquainted."

Joanna was left with little choice except to agree. As her uncle departed for the kitchen, she let her gaze swing to Linc Wilder. He was standing near the couch, watching her lazily with his cat's eyes.

Relegated to the role of hostess, she made a stiff gesture to invite him to sit down. "Make yourself comfortable."

"Thank you." Dryness quirked the corners of his mouth as he folded his long body onto the couch.

He removed his hat, setting it on the adjoining sofa cushion, and combed his fingers through the brown thickness of his hair to unflatten it. His glance ran back to her in a prodding reminder that she was still standing. Joanna sat down in the nearest chair, too nervous to relax against the seat back.

"So you were embarrassed yesterday?" It was a baiting question. "You didn't appear to be."

"No one likes to feel embarrassed. They usually try to cover it up with a show of indifference or bravado." She relied on those ploys now and attempted to put him on the defensive by questioning his actions the previous day. "You knew who I was. You probably even guessed Reece was my uncle before I mentioned it. Yet you didn't acknowledge that you knew him. Don't you think that was rude not to let me know how much farther it was to the cabin?"

"That wasn't rude. It was rural."

"Which means?" she bristled.

"Which means we aren't in the habit of turning the other cheek," he replied, his level gaze on her. "You didn't appreciate the help we gave you getting the car out of the ditch. So why should I help you again?"

"I did appreciate your help," Joanna insisted.

"You didn't show it," Linc Wilder countered. "Or were you trying to supposedly cover up your true feelings again?"

"Maybe I didn't sound properly grateful," she conceded stiffly. "But you weren't exactly a model of tact yourself. You can't say that you behaved like a gentleman."

"No, but I didn't see any lady in the vicinity either." His smooth reply was almost a slap in the face.

Joanna whitened. "I hope you don't expect me to apologize for yesterday."

"I expect nothing."

"Good, because Mr. Bates is the only one who deserves an apology from me," she stated with a cold glare.

An eyebrow was briefly lifted. "At least you recognize that," he murmured.

"I recognize a lot of things, Mr. Wilder." She was angry, controlling her temper and the volume of her voice with an effort. "I have already admitted that I'm not proud of the way I behaved yesterday, but that isn't good enough for you. I pity your wife for being married to such a hard, unforgiving man."

"You can save your pity. I'm not married," he replied.

"I can see why," Joanna declared.

Her uncle returned from the kitchen, carrying a tray with three coffee mugs on it. He set it down on the short cypress table in front of the sofa, not noticing the sudden silence that dominated the room. After he had handed each of them a mug, he sat on the couch with Linc.

"It is a lovely evening," Reece stated on a contented note. "Did you hear the whippoorwills outside a few minutes ago?"

"No. I must not have been listening," Linc's drawled reply indicated a lack of interest. Joanna didn't answer at all.

For the first time, Reece noticed the closed expressions both of them were wearing and began to suspect that all was not right. He also sensed there would be no conversation unless he carried it. "Joanna admired your home when we drove by it today, Linc," he offered as a gambit to draw both of them into the discussion.

"Did she? I'm flattered." But a strong thread of mockery ran through the reply.

Reece saw the way Joanna's lips tightened in a thin line, a sure sign of temper. "His house commands quite a fantastic view. You can see for miles. We will have to stop sometime so you can see it."

"It sounds lovely. I can hardly wait." She was equally taunting, cloaking it behind false politeness. As if this front of pleasantness was too difficult to maintain, she abruptly set her cup down and rose from the chair. "Excuse me, will you? If I want to reach my mother before she goes out for the evening, I need to phone her now. I have some things I want her to send." The last was added to Reece as an explanation for the phone call.

"Use the phone in the study so you can have some privacy." Reece straightened, out of deference to her sex, but Linc remained seated as she left the room and closed the door. Resuming his seat, Reece let the silence run between them before he finally spoke his thoughts, needing to know what was wrong. "There is friction between you and my niece. What has caused it?"

Linc's gaze swung to the study door, narrowing slightly, then he attempted a smile. "Maybe it would be better if we talked about something else."

"Is it something that happened yesterday?" Reece persisted with the subject, anxious to smooth out any differences between the two. "Joanna admitted to me that she had said some pretty unforgivable things. She is young and her temper is quick."

"And her tongue is sharp," Linc added. "And she's a little too big for her britches." His glance ran sideways to Reece. "Sorry, but you asked for my opinion."

"From the time Joanna was small, her mother —my sister-in-law—has attempted to run every minute of her life. It's natural that Joanna began to resent that and learn to stand up for herself." Reece sketched in a little of his niece's background so Linc could understand her present behavior. "She doesn't like being told what to do," he paused to eye Linc with a knowing look. "And you are used to telling people what to do."

"Message received," Linc acknowledged with a wry twist of his mouth. "But I still think she needs to be pushed on her backside. It takes falling on your rear end a few times before you appreciate landing on your feet."

"You may have a point," Reece chuckled at the piece of Ozark wisdom. "But you also have to admit she is an attractive girl."

"A very attractive woman," Linc agreed on a thoughtful note, then appeared restless, a little irritated. He drained his cup and set it on the tray. "Thanks for the coffee, Reece."

"You aren't leaving already," he protested as Linc pushed to his feet.

"Yes. Give my goodbyes to your niece. I've done enough damage for one night," he said.

"Come by again," Reece issued the long standing invitation again.

"Thanks, I will." Taking his hat, he carried it with him to the door and put it on as he walked out.

When the truck motor started up, Reece saw the doorknob to the study turning slowly. "It's safe to come out now, Joanna," he called to his niece, a faint light gleaming in his dark eyes. "He's gone."

It was several seconds before the door actually opened and Joanna emerged. Reece pretended not to notice the way her glance went immediately to the place where Linc had been sitting. "Linc said to pass along his goodbye. He wasn't able to stay longer. By the way, did you reach Elizabeth?"

"No." Actually she hadn't tried, but she didn't tell her uncle that. It would be akin to admitting cowardice. "It's just as well. It would take too long to mail the things to me anyway. I'll go shopping tomorrow in town and pick up the few things I'll need while I'm here."

"That sounds sensible," he agreed.

"Why did you tell me it was safe to come out just because Linc Wilder was gone?" She wanted to know.

"It was obvious the two of you had been exchanging blows," he stated. "You wanted to avoid him. That's why you decided to call your mother."

"I couldn't help it. I know you like him and if I had stayed in the room—" she began tightly.

"Yes, I was aware of the sparks flying," he smiled gently. "What happened yesterday?"

"He started giving me a lecture on my manners."

"Which you needed?" Reece suggested with a raised eyebrow.

"Even if I did, he had no right to tell me about it, and I told him so," she retorted.

"Joanna." He shook his head at her with affection. "Hasn't it occurred to you that you aren't the only one with a lot of pride?"

"Yes, a couple of times," she admitted grudgingly, then smiled. "How about a game of back-gammon?"

"Get the board and I'll pour some more cof-fee."

They played until nearly midnight with nei-ther one winding up a clear-cut winner although Reece did have the advantage.

Upstairs in the loft, Joanna undressed for bed. A cool breeze was whispering through the trees outside her window where a whippoorwill was making its plaintive call. After pulling on a nightgown, she folded down the bed's coverlet and used only the sheet. She switched off the bedside lamp to send the room into darkness.

Her thoughts roamed over the evening's events, spending too much time on Linc Wilder and the way his presence had unnerved her. Joanna turned on her side and punched the pillow beneath her head. She couldn't seem to get comfortable. Maybe it was her conscience that was troubling her. On that thought, she closed her eyes.

Chapter Six

Joanna leaned her head out of the opened car window to call to her uncle. "Are you sure you don't want to come with me? It might not be smart to trust me with this car. I could run into a mule."

"I trust you." Reece laughed from the doorway of the cabin. "I have some notes to go over. Later on this afternoon I plan to do a little fishing."

"You just don't want to be dragged around from store to store while I try on clothes," she accused.

"You're right." He waved to her and she waved back before shifting the luxury car into reverse to back out of the driveway. "Enjoy yourself!"

The big car made better going over the rough

road. As she neared the fork in the road where a lane turned off to Jessie Bates's cabin, she chewed her lip thoughtfully. It had been at the back of her mind since last night that she really should apologize to the man. She slowed the car and made the sharp turn onto the track leading to his cabin.

It was set a quarter of a mile back, deep in the woods that grew thickly all the way to the lake. All the buildings looked ancient—the log cabin, a shed, and a small barnlike structure, yet there was an absence of litter in the yard. It had a tidy and neat appearance, not at all what she had expected.

The two mules were standing head to tail inside an enclosure fenced with rough cedar posts. One turned its head to look at her, its big ears flopping at the flies, but it lost interest when she stepped out of the car. She was about to decide the owner wasn't home. Just then the barn door squealed open and the man emerged.

Nothing about him had changed. He appeared to be wearing the same pair of baggy overalls— or a pair just like them—and a faded blue work shirt. His dark hair was just as straggly and in need of a combing, yet he looked clean. When he saw her standing there, his bony face assumed a closed expression.

"I would have come to pay you for the repairs to your car," he declared tightly. "There was no call to come collectin'. I told you I pay ma' debts."

She had offended him again. "I didn't stop

because of that," she said quickly. "I always pay my debts, too, and I owe you an apology." When she paused, he tipped his head back and gave her a long, considering look.

"I'm sorry for the things I said about you and your mules the other day. I wish I could take them all back, but I can't change the fact that I said them. But I am sorry."

"I reckon I can overlook it. 'Course I can't speak for my mules," he said but there appeared to be a suggestion of a twinkle in his eyes even though his stern expression didn't change.

"Thank you." She smiled, a little relieved. "I want you to know that my uncle speaks very highly of you." She realized that she hadn't introduced herself, not formally. "My name is Joanna Morgan." She extended her hand to him.

He self-consciously wiped his on the back of his overalls before pumping her hand. "Pleased to meet you, Miss Morgan."

"You have a very nice place here—quiet and secluded." Joanna felt she should say something favorable about his place as she let her glance sweep around the surroundings once more.

"Well, it's home," he drawled. "I ain't interested in the luxuries of life but I shore wouldn't mind havin' some of the necessities, like indoor plumbin'. I'm getting tired of takin' a bath in the spring behind the house. That water gets awful blasted cold at times."

Her eyes widened slightly, noticing that his hair was damp and there was the smell of pine-soap clinging to his skin. He had just come from taking his bath. She was a little dazed to discover he was serious about not having running water. In these modern times, it sounded so unlikely that she had to ask.

"Do you mean you really don't have indoor plumbing?" Unconsciously her gaze swept the buildings again. She noticed the path worn through the trees leading behind the cabin. To an outhouse?

"No," he confirmed her suspicion. "I been thinkin' about gettin' some electricity. But I get to thinkin' that after that I'd be wantin' a stove, a refrigerator, and a television. Right now I don't want none of those things 'cause I don't have electricity. I decided I'm probably happier without it, 'cause I'm not wantin' those other things that I can't afford."

"How do you keep your food from spoiling?"

"I gotta springhouse. It keeps everythin' chilled just right an' you don't have to defrost it. Folks have been keepin' food in a springhouse for years," he explained.

"Oh." She had thought they had vanished with the advent of television. It was becoming clear what Reece had meant when he'd said Jessie Bates enjoyed being eccentric.

"Excuse me a minute, while I go in the house and get the money I owe ya'." He started to turn away to walk to the porch steps.

"Wait." Joanna caught at his arm, feeling the tensile strength of his wiry muscles beneath the thin fabric of his shirt sleeve. "I really would rather that you didn't pay it because I feel so badly about the way I behaved. Besides, there virtually wasn't any damage to the car—just the paint scratched in a few places. It doesn't amount to anything."

"It was my fault for pulling out on the road like that. I gotta pay," he insisted.

She was about to argue when she remembered her uncle's comment last night that other people had pride, too. "All right," she gave in. "Ten dollars should cover the damage."

"It won't take me but a minute to fetch it," he said. His spindly legs carried him swiftly over the ground and up the steps to the cabin's door.

Alone in the yard, Joanna studied the clearing and its primitive buildings. The rocky ground was scattered with clumps of grass stubbornly forcing their way through the inhospitable earth. Most were thin, spindly blades, but some grew tall and defiant.

There was a quiet here that wasn't really silent. The buzz of the flies and the stomping of a mule's hoof, the soft swish of its tail intermixed with the distant chatter of a squirrel in the woods and the trilling calls of birds. But all of them were subtle sounds, in harmony with the surroundings. Therefore, it was the quiet solitude of the place that made the strongest impression on Joanna, rather than its many inhabitants.

The slam of the screen door hit a strident note and her glance swung to the cabin and the scrawny man descending the porch steps. She noticed the several bills clasped between his long, bony fingers.

"Here you go." He handed the money to her. "Now we're square."

"Yes." Joanna wasn't about to insult him by counting it. So she folded the curling and age-worn bills and slipped them in the side pocket of her slacks, trying not to think about where it might have been stashed in his cabin. No doubt he had some secure and obscure hidey-hole for his valuables. "It's very quiet here. Doesn't it bother you not to have any neighbors living close by?"

"If I wanted people livin' on top of me, I'd have a place in town." He seemed to find her question a little foolish.

"How much land do you have here?" As soon as she asked, Joanna wondered if she was being too nosy, but her curiosity was quite innocent.

"Thare's no way of tellin' just how much land I got," he explained with a serious frown. "The homestead papers say I got forty acres. But forty acres of this hill land ain't like forty acres of any other land. If you was to roll it out flat, I might have three, four times as much land."

She tried to hold back a smile until she noticed the definite twinkle in his eyes. He had meant the remark to be amusing. The line of her mouth curved in obliging response.

"You do have a point," she agreed, the smile broadening. "I wouldn't want to walk it."

His head was tilted to the side in a gesture of

disagreement. "Now thare's advantages to walkin' in these hills. Walkin' on flat land would be just plumb borin', not to mention how tirin' it would be without a downhill to spell ya'."

Joanna laughed openly this time at his pearl of Ozark wit. "I hadn't thought of that," she admitted.

"It's hard for some people to look and see at the same time," Jessie Bates stated.

Joanna sobered, because she knew she was guilty of that. The other day on the road, she had looked at Jessie Bates and judged him to be poor and ignorant without taking the time to *see* his worth as a man.

"Yes, it is." She didn't add more because they both understood what was meant. Instead, Joanna made the initial move to take her leave. "I'm on my way into town. Is there anything I could pick up for you?"

There was silent approval in his look. "That's right neighborly of you to offer but I got all I need to hold me for a spell."

"I'd better be leaving. Thanks for being so understanding, Mr. Bates." Joanna spoke as she began to turn to walk to the Chrysler.

He walked along side her. "Like I said, we're all squared."

A cardinal swooped out of the trees, flying directly in front of Joanna. The sudden flash of red startled her. She took a half-step backward, laughing at herself when she realized it had only been a bird. Continuing toward the car, she glanced sideways at her companion.

"These woods seemed to be filled with cardinals," she remarked.

"Thare's a few," he nodded. There was the smallest pause before he continued. "Some hillfolks believe that when a redbird flies across a girl's path, it means she's gonna be kissed twice before nightfall."

She turned her head to look at him, wondering if he was pulling her leg. "Why would they believe that?"

"They tend to be a superstitious lot." He shrugged. "'Course, it's foolishness. I don't put any stock in such things myself."

"Neither do I," she agreed on a more decisive note, then lightly mocked the belief. "Besides, I don't even have a boyfriend here." Or elsewhere, at the moment.

"The superstition just says you're gonna be kissed twice. It don't say who's gonna do the kissin'. 'Could be someone you know, or someone you don't."

She paused as she opened the car door to look at him closely, a tiny frown creeping across her forehead. He had disclaimed any belief in the superstition, yet he was defending it. It seemed very contradictory to her. A little confused, she laughed it off and slipped behind the steering wheel.

"I'm supposed to be kissed twice before nightfall, huh?" Her wry smile was taunting with skepticism. "I'll let you know what happens."

There was a trace of a smile in his expression

as he shut her car door—an expression that appeared to contain some secret knowledge. She shook her head slightly as she started the car, unsure what to believe about the man. She turned the car around in the yard to drive out the lane, waving to the man.

All the way to town her mind kept wandering back to the conversation. It was certainly something she would have to remember to tell her uncle. She knew he'd find it amusing, and interesting.

With the unscheduled stop at Jessie Bates's cabin and the traffic on the highway, it was nearly eleven by the time she reached town. She found a place to park on the main street. There were several nice dress shops within the block and Joanna entered the closest one first to look over their selection.

Despite her growing hunger, she shopped through the lunch hour while the stores were less crowded. At half-past one, she went in search of a restaurant. Two of the small cafes in town were filled with people waiting to be seated. At the third one, there was no one waiting in line although all the tables and booths were filled.

Since she wasn't sure if she'd have better luck elsewhere, Joanna decided to wait until there was a place. As she shifted the packages under her arm, her glance absently swept the room.

A woman was seated alone at a table for four. It was Rachel Parmelee. As Joanna recognized her, the woman happened to look up straight at Joanna. Joanna smiled in acknowledgment but the widow looked right through her.

Although it was possible Rachel Parmelee was too preoccupied with her own thoughts to notice Joanna or else she honestly didn't recognize her, it was also possible she was deliberately ignoring her. Remembering how cool and unfriendly the widow had become toward her uncle prompted Joanna to force the issue. She walked to the table for four where the woman was seated.

"Good afternoon, Mrs. Parmelee." There was a slight challenge in her smile as she stopped beside one of the empty chairs at the table.

The woman looked up, a little too blank. "Good afternoon." Again there was a surface pleasantness that didn't truly welcome.

"I'm Joanna Morgan. We met yesterday in your shop," she reminded the woman of their previous introduction.

"Yes, of course. How are you, Miss Morgan?" The polite inquiry was just that and nothing more.

"Fine, thank you." The less welcome she was made to feel, the more determined Joanna became to stay. "The rest of the tables are full. Would you mind if I sat with you?"

Without waiting for an invitation, Joanna deposited her packages on the empty seat of a chair and sat down in the one opposite the widow. Not even Rachel Parmelee could be so rude as to refuse the request and Joanna knew it.

"Please do," the woman murmured after the fact.

The waitress stopped at their table with a glass of water and a menu for Joanna and a diet plate consisting of tomato slices, cottage cheese, and a hamburger patty for Rachel Parmelee. The waitress left, promising to be back to take Joanna's order. She opened the menu and pretended to study the bill of fare.

"Do you eat here regularly, Mrs. Parmelee?" Joanna inquired as she continued to peruse the menu.

"Yes."

"I suppose it takes too much time to run home every day and fix lunch for yourself when you have a business to run," she suggested.

"Yes."

"Myself, I never eat breakfast in the morning so by noontime, I'm starving," Joanna chattered away, deliberately keeping the conversation going in opposition to the woman's one-word answers. "Everything on the menu looks good. What would you recommend?"

"All restaurant food has begun to taste alike for me." Rachel Parmelee disqualified herself as the person to ask. "The restaurant has a good reputation in the area so I'm sure anything you choose would be satisfactory."

"That's good to know." Joanna contained a smug smile at the longer reply she had forced from the widow. The waitress returned to the table to take her order, diverting Joanna's attention for the moment. "I'll have the beef and noodles, and a glass of iced tea, please." When the waitress left, Joanna let a rueful smile touch her mouth. "I'll probably regret eating so much later on when I start trying on clothes again."

"Really?" Rachel murmured, displaying little interest.

"Yes. It's been a long time since I've been on a shopping spree. I'm really enjoying it," she explained. "Reece decided he'd rather stay at the cabin than follow me around while I shop."

"I'm sure."

Joanna couldn't help noticing the way the widow seemed to freeze up when she mentioned Reece's name. "The stores here seem to carry a quality brand of clothes. Now I know why you always look so well dressed. Where do you shop locally?" Joanna knew few members of her own sex who were not willing to talk about clothes.

"Several places. I don't patronize any one store. As a rule, I make my own," Rachel stated, removing herself from any discussion about the relative merits of one shop over another.

"As busy as you are, I'm surprised you find the time to sew," Joanna murmured dryly.

"After a long day, it helps me to relax although the bulk of my sewing I do in the winter when business is slower," she admitted.

Joanna ran an appraising eye over the smartly tailored suit of cool mint seersucker. "That's an attractive outfit you're wearing. Did you make it?"

"Yes."

"With a business to run, I don't imagine you have a chance to go out much—socially." She surmised the reason Rachel had turned down Reece's invitations.

"No. It keeps me very busy." Again there was a stiffness in the reply. "I don't mind it a bit. I prefer to be independent rather than to rely on someone else to support me."

Joanna had the vague impression there was some kind of a dig in the last statement. "I must admit I agree with your philosophy."

This time Rachel didn't make any comment at all to Joanna's remark. Again she sensed that it was the mention of Reece. But why? If only she could get the woman to open up, maybe she would learn something. With an inner sigh, Joanna returned to the only safe topic she knew —the woman's pride in her business.

"From what I saw the other day, your shop seems to be very successful. That can't happen without a good deal of time and effort."

"It has taken several years to establish a reputation and acquire a clientele that keeps coming back," Rachel agreed that it had required an effort.

"How long have you had the store?" she asked. "I know it's been more than six years, because Reece bought me a Kewpie doll. At the time, I wasn't overly enthused about it. I was trying so hard to be accepted as an adult and here was my uncle bringing me a child's gift—or so I thought at the time."

"He is your uncle?" The question appeared to be startled from Rachel, a wary and surprised look in her eyes.

"Of course, he's my uncle," Joanna laughed with some surprise at the question and noticed the sudden flush that colored the woman's cheeks. "Who did you think he was?"

"I'm sorry. Of course I knew he was your uncle." Rachel insisted forcefully and did an excellent job of recovering her poise.

It was beginning to register what the widow had thought. "You didn't believe I was his niece, did you?" she accused thoughtfully. "You had convinced yourself I was his lover masquerading as his niece for the sake of propriety."

"Is it so illogical?" Rachel no longer attempted to deny it. "Your uncle is an extraordinarily charming man, wealthy—sophisticated. It isn't that unlikely he would have a young mistress, is it?"

"It isn't unlikely," Joanna admitted. "But it doesn't happen to be true either. And I doubt very much if Reece would try to hide the fact. If he cared enough about a woman to have an affair with her, he certainly wouldn't treat her with the disrespect of a false claim that they were related. He simply isn't made that way."

"I don't know your uncle all that well," Rachel asserted in defense of her wrong conclusion.

"From what I can gather, it's your fault that the two of you haven't become better acquainted," Joanna murmured.

She lowered her gaze, losing her air of self-containment. Joanna was startled to see how unsure the widow seemed, almost vulnerable. But her voice was steady when she replied to Joanna's subtle jibe.

"Considering the circumstances, there has hardly been time to become acquainted with your uncle. Running my business requires most of my hours and the summer is my busiest season. I barely have time for close friends and your uncle is only here one month of the year. That is hardly the basis for a stable relationship, even discounting the fact that we have nothing in common."

"Nothing in common," Joanna repeated, a little puzzled. "It would seem to me that you have several things in common, not the least among them would be that you both own and manage your own company."

"Please, Miss Morgan," the widow protested in a scathing tone. "Let's not pretend that my little store in any way compares to the large organization Reece runs. He lives in a sophisticated world of high finance and I'm just a little shopkeeper. We hardly travel in the same circles."

"I don't think we're talking about the same person," Joanna said with a vaguely amused look. "The man you are describing would be vacationing in the South of France, not the Ozark Mountains of Missouri."

Rachel Parmelee was plainly at a loss to argue

that point although her mouth opened on several attempts. "Perhaps," she said finally and appeared discomfitted by the admission.

Letting instinct guide her, Joanna asked a question that seemed to be off the subject, but the inner workings of her mind were already plotting a use for the answer. "You surely don't work seven days a week at the store, do you? I should think it would be impossible to keep up a pace like that."

It took a second for the widow to adjust to the apparent change of subject. "No. Since the weekends are generally our busiest time, I take off on Friday to rest up for them."

"You mentioned that you'd lost your taste for restaurant food. Why don't you have dinner with us Friday night and enjoy a home-cooked meal for a change?" The invitation bordered on a challenge. Rachel's initial reaction was what Joanna had expected—refusal.

"No." She seemed to struggle to find an acceptable excuse. "I'll be too busy. It's the only time I have to wash clothes and clean. I—"

"This way you won't have to worry about fixing a meal," Joanna reasoned.

Rachel abandoned her pretence. "I know what you're trying to do and it just won't work," she insisted. "After five minutes with your uncle, I run out of things to say."

The remark confirmed Joanna's suspicions that the widow's coolness was an attempt to conceal she felt awkward and self-conscious with Reece. "So?" She made light of it. "If that happens, you can talk to me instead. Will you come?" She watched the hesitation and indecision in the woman's face. "You have nothing to lose—and, maybe, everything to gain," she prodded softly.

A very human expression took over Rachel's features as she yielded to the temptation. "All right, I'll come," she agreed and smiled a little foolishly. "I'm probably making a big mistake."

Satisfaction swelled inside Joanna until she thought she would burst, but she managed to contain most of it. "Look on the bright side," she reasoned. "You can always blame me and say I told you so."

The waitress came to the table with Joanna's order. She glanced at the widow. "Was there anything else you wanted, Rachel?"

The query seemed to prompt Rachel Parmelee to glance at her watch. "No." She was surprised at the time that had passed. "I have to get back to the store. It's much later than I realized."

"Do you know where we're staying?" Joanna asked as the woman gathered up her purse and her luncheon check.

"Yes, I do." She still didn't look positive that she had been right in accepting the invitation.

"Dinner will be ready at seven on Friday. You can come at six or six-thirty—any time you like," Joanna said. "We'll be expecting you."

"Friday at seven." There was a responding nod.

As Rachel walked to the cashier, Joanna couldn't help feeling very pleased with herself.

The sheer fact that Rachel had accepted the invitation indicated that she was attracted to Reece. Joanna really hadn't needed to twist her arm that much. She could hardly wait to see Reece's face when she told him Rachel was coming to dinner.

Chapter Seven

$\mathscr{I}$t was late afternoon by the time Joanna had finished her shopping and returned to the cabin by the lake. Her uncle wasn't on hand to greet her. A note on the table reminded her that he had gone fishing. In her excitement to relay the day's momentous events to him, it had slipped her mind that he'd mentioned his fishing plans when she'd left in the morning.

It was a letdown to have to wait to tell him about what had happened. She carried her packages up the stairs to the loft bedroom where she removed the price tags from the garments she'd purchased.

The windows were opened to admit any breeze but there wasn't a breath of air stirring. All the afternoon heat seemed to have gathered in the second floor of the cabin, stifling in its staleness and humidity. Perspiration trickled down her neck as she hung the new clothes in the closet.

By the time she was through, she was hot and sticky. She was considering a shower when she glanced out the bedroom window and saw the beckoning waters of the lake. Splashing around in it sounded infinitely more refreshing than a cool shower. In five minutes, Joanna had changed into her turquoise green swimsuit and grabbed a terrycloth beach jacket and towel.

She didn't bother with sandals, which she regretted seconds after stepping off the back porch onto the gravel-based earth. Unable to face the thought of climbing those stairs back to the stifling heat of the second floor for the sandals, Joanna minced her way across the stony ground barefoot to the lake shore.

Leaving her jacket and towel on a limestone ledge, she waded into the water, its coolness almost shocking her hot skin. When the water reached her waist, she pushed off to begin a leisurely crawl.

Linc climbed out of the cab of his truck and paused to stare at the log cabin. He wasn't entirely sure of his motive for stopping, except that he'd been drawn here after Jessie's revelation to him that Joanna had stopped to apologize. It didn't make a lot of sense why that mattered and the prospect of delving too deeply into the reason why it did made him uncomfortable.

The cabin looked quiet and unoccupied. His glance went again to the New Yorker parked near his truck. Its presence confirmed the cabin's inhabitants had not left. With a little shrug to rid himself of his brief indecision, Linc walked to the door and knocked. The screen door rattled in its frame at the pounding while the wire mesh kept him from seeing anything more than shadowy forms inside the cabin.

No sounds came from inside to indicate his knock had been heard. He started to knock again, then changed his mind, opening the door instead.

"Hello! Anybody home!" His voice seemed to echo through the empty house as silence answered him. Linc walked in, letting the door close behind him. "Reece?"

Nothing. He crossed the living room to the screened door leading onto the back porch. His gaze, always alert to his surroundings, moved absently about the room. It ran automatically to the large window that overlooked the lake and its shore, since that was where he suspected the occupants of this home were. Linc paused when he noticed the boat wasn't beached on the shore, reaching the conclusion that Reece had obviously gone fishing and probably taken Joanna with him.

He would have turned around and left if he hadn't glimpsed some movement in his side vision. When he looked to see what it was, he forgot all about leaving. Joanna was wading ashore, her sun-golden limbs glistening.

The jewel-colored swimsuit was molded to her figure like a second skin, boldly outlining the jutting swell of her breasts and the curve of her firm hips. He was conscious of the quickening rush that disturbed his senses, proving he was vulnerable to the attractions of a shapely body—if he had any doubts.

She picked her way along the rocky shoreline to a ledge of rock. Linc watched from the window while she toweled dry and rubbed the dampness from her honey-dark hair. There was a supple grace to her movements, a natural earthiness that was innocently sexy.

It didn't occur to him to go to the porch door and alert her to his presence. He was content to leave her unaware that she was being observed while his mind played back its impressions of their previous meetings and coupled them with the facts he'd learned about her from Reece. She had aroused his interest as few women had these past years.

When she slipped on her beach jacket without bothering to tie the front closed and started toward the cabin, Linc reached in his pocket for a cigarette, lighting it and shaking out the match although he continued to hold it between his fingers.

Everything about him—his stance, his posture —indicated disinterest toward the blonde girl approaching the cabin—everything except his eyes. They were alive to her, watching as she picked her way, barefoot, over the rough ground.

In spite of himself—it seemed—Linc was stirred by the freshness of her beauty and the intelligence that was such an integral part of her features. Although she had the face, the figure, and the coloring for it, there was nothing about her that suggested a dumb blonde. The more he learned about her, the more she seemed to challenge him.

When she climbed the steps to the porch, Linc half-turned so he would be facing the door when she entered the cabin. Her lips lay against each other in a relaxed curve of contentment as she crossed the threshold and paused to close the screen door, the towel swinging in one hand.

Joanna didn't immediately see him standing there. Something warned her of his presence before her eyes made the adjustment from bright sunlight to shade. Perhaps it was the smell of cigarette smoke or a faint sound. It might have been some sixth sense that alerted her to him.

When she saw him standing there, so motionless and catlike in his quiet study of her, her heart did a somersault and never properly regained its former location. This failure was concealed by the quick erection of her defenses. Joanna had long ago learned that sometimes the best way to defend herself was to attack.

"How did you get in here?" Her voice was husky.

"Sorry, I didn't mean to startle you. I knocked

but no one answered," Linc Wilder explained somewhat casually. Joanna watched him toss a burned-out match into an ashtray.

"No one answered the door and you walked in anyway?" She made it a challenge, conscious of the uneven hammering of her pulse under the steady regard of his tawny eyes.

They gleamed with amusement and the corners of his mouth lifted. "Since the car was outside, I presumed someone was here. I figured you or Reece were down by the lake so I took the liberty of taking a shortcut through the cabin instead of walking around it. I happened to see you from the window when you were walking up from the lake so I waited here."

He made it all sound very plausible, which Joanna supposed it was. It was just that she felt so awkward and self-conscious whenever she was around him, probably because she hadn't made a very good first impression. But she didn't want to admit that it mattered, especially not to him.

"Why are you here?" she demanded. "If you came to see Reece, he's fishing. You can come back later or leave a message for him."

"I didn't stop to see Reece."

The statement caught her off guard. Her hand crept up to close the front of her jacket. She was suddenly conscious of her scanty attire and wasn't sure whether it had been caused by the lick of his downward glance or the touch of a light breeze from outside.

"I can't think why you would want to see me. I

don't want to see you," she said with an attempt at callous indifference and turned away to walk to the kitchen. She could hear the even tread of his footsteps above the silent patter of her own bare feet as he followed her as far as the doorway and stopped.

"Jessie Bates mentioned you stopped to see him this morning." His statement seemed to contain a request for an explanation.

"So?" Joanna opened the refrigerator door to take out the pitcher of lemonade. Since he showed no signs of leaving, it would have been rude not to offer him some refreshment. "Would you like a glass?" She threw him a glance over her shoulder.

"Yes, thank you." He waited until she had poured a glass for each of them and was crossing the kitchen to the doorway where he stood. "He also told me that you apologized to him."

"I did." Joanna held out a glass to him. He took it, then turned aside so she could pass. "I told you I owed him an apology. Didn't you believe that I actually meant to tell him?" Her senses reacted to the brief seconds of closeness when she moved by him.

"I guess I was wondering whether you went on your own or if Reece suggested it," Linc replied.

Joanna pivoted a little sharply, the lemonade sloshing in her glass. "I didn't get around to telling Reece my intentions. He doesn't even know about it yet, so you can stop wondering," she retorted.

It was difficult to hold his look, so she sought a

chair. Sitting down, Joanna crossed her long legs and struggled for that cool sophistication her mother had worked so hard to instill in her. On the surface, she appeared to achieve it. Linc crushed out his cigarette in an ashtray and continued to stand.

"I decided it was better to ask the question than to arrive at any more hasty conclusions," he said.

"Are you having doubts that I might not be the spoiled, ill-mannered brat you thought I was?" she mocked him.

"It's possible you might even be human." The devilish light in his eyes taunted her.

"The next thing you know you'll be admitting I have feelings," Joanna warned him lightly.

"I might even concede there were extenuating circumstances for your behavior," Linc suggested.

"I don't know if I could take the shock," she countered.

"Then let's just say you've improved my opinion of you." A half-smile slanted his mouth, crooking it in an attractive manner.

She was stiffened by the feeling that she had to guard against liking him or end up being hurt. It brought a dryness to her voice. "I'd ask what that opinion is, but I don't think I would like it."

"Why?" Her reply sharpened his interest.

"Probably because you strike me as the type who believes women belong in the home." She gave him a cool look. "Isn't it the motto of the hills to keep them barefoot and pregnant?"

"Are you for it or against it?"

"Against it, of course," she flashed. "It's old-fashioned and ridiculous. Why?" She was suddenly suspicious of the apparent innocence of his question.

"I thought you might be planning to go native. I notice you're barefoot but I didn't know if you were pregnant, too." The golden flecks in his eyes were dancing with pure mockery.

Her stomach was churning with a violent emotion, which she believed was akin to anger. She pushed to her feet, discarding the lemonade glass on a side table, not trusting her hand to hold it and not throw it in his face.

"I'm not going native and I'm not pregnant. I was swimming as you very well know." She was on the verge of losing her temper, and was shaking with the effort to keep it under control. "I'm not going to turn myself into a baby factory for any man."

Linc tipped his head to one side. "Has someone asked?"

Joanna realized that she had allowed his remarks to grow out of all proportion. She was suddenly embarrassed and at a loss for words. Aware of her reddening cheeks, she held her head a little higher.

"I don't see any point in continuing this conversation," she declared on a note of pride, and would have swept past him in a grand exit, but his hand caught her arm.

Joanna stopped at the contact, before any pressure had been exerted to halt her. As a result, she was positioned to one side of him. She didn't turn her head to look at him, but merely swung her gaze, elevating its angle the necessary degrees to center on his rough-hewn features.

"Did you lose your sense of humor again?" His low voice was rich and smooth with amusement. "You are very sensitive, aren't you? Your pride is easily pricked even though you pretend to have a thick skin."

She had been accused of a lot of things by various men friends but none had ever suggested she was sensitive or easily hurt. Her gaze wavered under the probing inspection of his eyes. Joanna let it fall to the hand on her bare forearm, sun-tanned and strong. Its easy touch managed to hint at the potential of power in his grip. A warmth radiated from it, sensitizing her skin.

"Do you know what your problem is, Joanna?" Linc's all-knowing tone provoked a response.

"No, but I'm sure you're going to tell me whether I want to hear it or not," she retorted acidly.

When she lifted her gaze to his face, she saw that her remark had transmitted very little of its sting. The fanning lines at the corners of his eyes were crinkled in silent laughter.

"You always want to have the upper hand in a conversation. The minute you lose control, you run." A trace of wryness flitted across his expression. "You can dish it out but you can't take it."

"Is that right?" Joanna attempted to mock him but it sounded weak even to her.

She was nervous and on edge, trembling from an inner turmoil she couldn't define. She wanted to escape this conversation, but how could she after what Linc had just said? A little desperately, she tore her gaze from his face to search the room as if something in it would provide an excuse.

"Why are you frightened?" Linc asked with a steadiness that started a flood of panic.

"That's ridiculous! I'm not frightened of anything," Joanna denied and started to twist away from the loose grip of his hand.

But he shifted his hold, changing it from her arm to the curve of her waist and turning her as he turned so they were squarely facing each other. When that was accomplished, he cupped a large hand to the side of her neck where her pulse was visibly throbbing.

"Aren't you?" he challenged quietly. "Then why are you trembling?"

"I'm not," she lied.

Her hands were braced against his waistline to maintain the space between them, but he was so close that she could see the individual flecks of gold in his light brown eyes and the masculine texture of his skin stretched across his angular features, shadowed slightly by the shaven growth of his beard.

She was conscious of his flatly muscled stomach and the width of his shoulders and chest. With each breath, she was inhaling the tang of tobacco smoke that blended with the natural odor of his body, a combination that seemed to stimulate her senses. Joanna wasn't comfortable with the way he was affecting her.

"Are you afraid of sex?" His seemingly idle question skyrocketed her pulse, turning her thoughts in a direction she didn't want them to take.

The hand on her neck moved, showing disinterest in the rapid escalation of her pulse as his fingers absently traced the underside of her jaw and paused to let his thumb rub the point of her chin.

"Sex is a normal, biological function. Every living thing is designed to reproduce through one method or another. The birds and the bees do it. The human species is gifted with the capacity to enjoy it."

She was distracted by his reference to birds, the single word triggering her memory. When he lowered his mouth onto hers, her lips parted in surprise. There was nothing hesitant about his kiss, nothing tentative or uncertain. Yet neither was there force. The pressure of his mouth was warm and firm against hers, moving over her lips and tasting their natural softness.

His fingers tunneled into her hair to support the back of her neck. Brute strength she could have fought, but not this tantalizing possession that seemed to seek no more than a mutual enjoyment of the experience.

Was that true? Or was she subconsciously being influenced by primitive superstition into believing this kiss was inevitable because it had been foretold by an omen? His mouth eased from her lips and began to graze slowly along her smooth cheek.

"Did Jessie Bates put you up to this?" There was a disturbed level to her voice that proved she wasn't unaffected by this kiss. The stirring warmth of his breath against her lashes kept her eyes closed.

"Jessie?" He lifted his head an inch or two, a puzzled frown arching a dark brow. Joanna risked a glance at him and saw the vague bemusement in his eyes. "What has he got to do with this?"

"He arranged this with you so I would be kissed before nightfall and fulfill his silly prophecy because that bird flew in front of me," she accused in a none too steady voice.

There was a brief, negative movement of his head. "Jessie didn't mention anything to me about birds or kisses but if that's what he said, I don't want to make a liar out of him," Linc murmured huskily.

His mouth took hers again with familiar ease. There was a subtle difference in its possession, a quality of probing hunger in his kiss that seemed to test her ability to satisfy him. Her response to the silent challenge was almost involuntary as a melting warmth spread over her body.

His arms were around her, his hands gliding along her spine and applying casual pressure to arch her to his length. Her own fingers were splayed across the back of his ribcage, feeling the hard sinewed flesh and the body heat that flowed through the material of his shirt.

There was a traitorous excitement building in her system. Her hold on reality was weakening under the dizzying rush of emotion aroused by his experienced advance. Joanna became conscious of the scrape of rough denim against the bareness of her thighs and legs as she leaned against the solid support of his hips. The western buckle of his belt was poking her ribs and she realized her beach jacket was hanging open.

She was frightened by the part of her that wanted this intimacy to continue and grow, yet she lacked the determination and willpower to end the kiss. It was up to Linc to bring it to a gradual conclusion, which he did.

The instant her mouth was free of his possession, Joanna lowered her chin. There seemed to be so little air in her lungs. She struggled not to drink it in in gulps, not wanting Linc to know how breathless his kiss had left her. She brought her hands around to rest against his chest and establish space between them while still taking advantage of his support.

"Now you can tell Jessie that his prediction came true." With a slight toss of her head, Joanna met his heavily lidded gaze and attempted to show her indifference of him.

But she had the uneasy feeling those eyes saw right through her pretence. When his head began to descend toward her, she turned her face aside to avoid another kiss and stiffened her arms. Linc didn't try to hold her when she pushed out of his embrace and took a couple of steps to put distance between them.

"No more, Linc." She forced out a short laugh as she tried to treat the incident as a humorous experiment. "Jessie predicted I would only be kissed twice. As you said, we don't want to make a liar out of him."

When she turned around to look at him, his narrowed gaze slowly traveled down the length of her body, lingering on the exposed swell of her breasts revealed by the daring cut of her bathing suit and on the tanned bareness of her long legs. The boldness of his look brought a draining rush of heat through her body.

Her hands were shaking as she quickly wrapped the front of her terrycloth jacket closed and tied its sash in a tight knot. Flustered by the physical effect he was having on her, Joanna half-turned away. Purely by chance, she faced the screen door to the back porch. Through its dark mesh, she saw a figure approaching the cabin.

"Joanna—" Linc spoke her name, a summons in its pitch.

"Here comes Reece." She leaped on the excuse to ignore him and took long, swift steps to reach the screen door. She pushed it open and called to her uncle. "Hi! Did you catch any fish?"

"None." There was little disappointment in either his voice or his expression as he climbed the steps to the porch. "I had a few nibbles, but that's all. They'll probably start biting closer to evening."

Reece paused to set his fishing rod and reel against the outside of the cabin along with his tackle box before he moved to the door she was holding open for him. His glance took in the beach jacket she was wearing and the bareness of her legs.

"You've been swimming, I see," he observed as he crossed the threshold. Almost immediately he noticed their visitor. "Well, hello, Linc." His quick smile revealed his pleasure at seeing the man. "Have you been here long?"

"He arrived a few minutes ago," Joanna answered before Linc could.

"Yes." Linc went along with her answer and added a comment of his own. "Joanna has been entertaining me."

She knew precisely what he meant by his mocking insinuation and was glad it escaped her uncle. As she became aware of sudden quiet that had fallen, she noticed Reece dart her a sharp glance before his gaze returned to Linc. That's when she saw what had caught her uncle's eyes. The front of Linc's shirt was damp where it had absorbed the moisture from her wet swimsuit. Fortunately her uncle was too tactful to mention it.

"Was there something special you wanted to see me about?" he asked Linc.

"No. I just stopped to say hello." Linc assured him there was no other purpose behind his visit other than a friendly one.

"Since you're here, why don't you stay for dinner?" Reece invited.

"No thanks."

"That reminds me," Joanna inserted quickly before her uncle could pursue that topic and possibly change Linc's mind. "I had lunch with Rachel Parmelee today."

It was a subject guaranteed to attract her uncle's undivided attention. She saw the quick eagerness leap into his expression and light his dark eyes. The mere mention of her name brought an added warmth to his smile.

"Did you? How was she?" He tried to disguise his avid interest, but wasn't too successful.

"Fine." Joanna paused to add impetus to her next statement. "I invited her to dinner Friday night." She waited for the rush of elation in his expression but it never came. Instead he became guarded.

"Did she accept?" he questioned.

"Yes," she assured him, pleased with her success. "It took a little persuading, but she finally agreed to come."

It was several seconds before Reece said a rather bland, "Good." It left her slightly stunned. She had expected him to rejoice at the news but he had practically no positive reaction at all. She was too confused to protest when he turned to Linc and asked, "Will you join us for dinner Friday evening to even out the numbers?"

"It would be my pleasure," Linc accepted.

"What time did you tell Rachel?" he inquired with a glance at Joanna.

"I said dinner would be at seven and for her to

come any time before that," she replied as confusion drew lines in her expression. "I thought you would prefer to contact her and make arrangements to pick her up."

"Would you object to bringing Mrs. Parmelee, Linc?" Reece asked.

Like Joanna, Linc appeared slightly puzzled by the request, too. "If that's what you want," he agreed to it.

"Thank you."

There appeared to be a great many unanswered questions in Linc's eyes when he studied his friend but he didn't ask one of them. Instead he made his excuse to leave. "I'd better be getting back to the place."

"It was good to see you, Linc." For once her uncle didn't attempt to persuade him to stay or protest that it was early.

A fact that didn't escape Linc's notice either. "I'll see you on Friday." His glance held hers for an instant. "Joanna," he nodded in her direction before moving toward the front door.

When it closed behind him, she looked back at her uncle, still puzzled by his behavior. He seemed to deliberately avoid her eyes and assumed a preoccupation that indicated he had a great many important matters on his mind.

"Would you mind fixing the meal tonight, Joanna?" It was more in the order of a request than a question. "I have some things I must do. I'll be in the study."

As he started to walk away without waiting for a response, she frowned and shook her head. "I don't understand you," she declared on a heavy breath of exasperation.

"Is something wrong?" His arched glance was too smooth.

"Something is, but I don't know what," she admitted and went to the heart of the matter. "Aren't you *glad* Rachel is coming for dinner?"

"Of course." Again there was an unnatural ease to his reply that completely lacked expression. "Are you upset because I invited Linc? Haven't the two of you patched up your differences yet?" His tone made it plain that he believed they had.

Joanna wouldn't be sidetracked from the real issue. "I don't care if he comes but I thought you'd welcome the chance to be alone with Rachel."

"It was your invitation she accepted, not mine," he stated.

That was the crux of the matter. Her mouth dropped open at this discovery her uncle was jealous that she had succeeded where he had failed. He disappeared into the study while she was still trying to find her voice.

Chapter Eight

Later on that evening, Joanna had the opportunity to explain to her uncle how the dinner invitation had come about and the reason she had been successful in persuading Rachel Parmelee to come. It had been a very one-sided conversation with Reece offering no comment and asking no questions. When it was over, she wasn't entirely sure that she had convinced him Rachel Parmelee's sole reason for accepting was based on a desire to spend the evening with him.

Ever since, he had been moody and preoccupied most of the time. He wasn't himself at all. Everything was left up to Joanna. He didn't offer any suggestions for the menu or help in any of the advance preparations for the meal.

The spinach salad was in the refrigerator

along with the trout in its broiling pan, ready to be slipped under the broiler. The potatoes were baking in the oven and the broccoli sat in its steaming pan on the range, while the peach cobbler cooled on a wire rack. Joanna checked it all one last time before entering the living room where she had set the table, complete with a white linen cloth, candles, and the best glass and silverware she could find.

The living room was too well lit, so she began a circuit of the room shutting off unnecessary lamps and leaving a strategic few on to create a more intimate atmosphere. The porch door opened and closed. Aware it was her uncle, Joanna didn't bother to look around.

"What are you doing?" he asked.

"There were too many lights on." She stopped beside the fireplace and a trace of regret flitted across her expression. "It's a pity it's July. It would be nice to have a fire blazing away." Then she turned and smiled quickly. "You look very handsome tonight."

Which he did. There was a casual sophistication to his simple attire of a plain silk shirt and dark slacks. It enhanced the silvered darkness of his hair and eyes, the leanness of his build.

He returned the compliment. "You look very lovely in that dress. Is it new?"

Reflex caused her to glance at the china blue tunic-style dress of crepe de chine, belted at the waist. It had an understated elegance to its basic style. She smoothed a hand over the practically wrinkle-free material.

"It's one I brought with me," she explained.

When she looked up, she saw that he had once again become preoccupied. His attention was away from her as his glance skimmed the table set for four.

"You shouldn't have gone to so much trouble," he said flatly.

"Why not? It's a special occasion," Joanna insisted.

He glanced briefly at his gold watch. "She isn't coming."

Reece sounded so positive that, for an instant, Joanna thought Rachel might have telephoned to cancel the invitation, but she hadn't heard the phone ring. She glanced at the wall clock above the kitchen cupboards, just visible through the archway, and saw it was half past six.

"The traffic is probably holding them up." She found an excuse to explain why Rachel Parmelee and Linc hadn't arrived yet.

"She won't come," he repeated. "You'll see." He walked to the window to gaze at the lake, the lowering rays of the sun reflecting off its mirror surface.

Joanna sighed, but didn't try to argue with him.

The car traveled at a reduced speed over the rutted gravel road. Rachel Parmelee sat as stiff as a statue in the passenger seat, rarely looking to the right or left. Her hands were clasped tightly on the clutch purse in her lap, the knuckles of her fingers showing white. Tension was written all over her expression.

"It's less than a mile now," Linc informed her.

On the drive here, they had talked about everything but their destination. The weather had been discussed at great length; this summer's trade had been compared to last year's.

"I shouldn't have come," Rachel blurted out the thought that had been on her mind ever since Linc had picked her up. She was embarrassed to discover she'd said it aloud.

"It's too late to turn back now," he replied evenly.

"I'm sorry," she apologized for her lack of poise. "I must sound like a silly schoolgirl on her first date." That was the way she felt, painfully nervous and awkward, her stomach churning. It was absurd to be so close to tears.

"There's no reason to be nervous." There was gentle humor in the warm look Linc Wilder gave her. "Reece won't bite—at least not on the first date."

In her present agitation, the remark was hardly laughable. "I can't help feeling that I'm out of my league," she sighed. "Here I am in a dress I made myself when he's used to taking out fashion models in designer clothes."

"I have known Reece for ten years. He isn't the kind of man who judges a person's worth by the label on their clothes." He applied the brake and made the turn into the cabin's driveway.

Stopping the car, he switched off the engine

and glanced at his passenger. She sat frozen in her seat while he climbed out of the car and walked around to open her door. Her hands were like ice when he helped her out of the car and closed the door.

Inside the cabin, Joanna had heard the car drive in and the first door being slammed shut. She unconsciously held her breath until she heard the second, half-afraid Reece might be right and Rachel Parmelee would back out at the last minute.

"They have arrived." She stressed the plural slightly and glanced at her uncle to see his reaction.

But he continued to stare out the window at the lake. Joanna sighed, wanting to shake him. At the rap on the door, she crossed the room to admit their guests. She pushed open the screen door and smiled warmly.

"Come in. I see Linc managed to get you here safely," she said addressing her comments to Rachel and ignoring Linc—on the surface. An inner radar was completely sensitive to his presence. "Was the traffic very heavy?"

"No." Even as the widow entered the cabin, her gaze was racing past Joanna.

A hint of pink appeared in the woman's cheeks, almost a match to the pale pink dress she was wearing. Joanna stole a look over her shoulder, already guessing the cause for the widow's faint blush.

Reece was standing near the center of the living room, waiting to greet their guests. Joanna wished he would smile and get rid of that proudly courteous look.

"Hello, Reece," Rachel greeted him in a stilted fashion.

"Good evening, Rachel," he responded in a like manner.

They both sounded so formal that Joanna wouldn't have been surprised if he'd made a stiff and courtly bow over the widow's hand. Her mouth tightened.

"I think it's going to be cool tonight," Linc murmured as he paused beside her.

She flashed him a glance that said she knew exactly what he meant. Although when his hand moved to the hollow of her back to guide her into the room with the others, she felt anything but cool. She shifted away from his touch at the first opportunity.

"Make yourselves comfortable," she urged and excused herself. "I have to check on dinner. Why don't you offer them a drink, Reece?"

"What would you like?" her uncle inquired of his guests while Joanna retreated to the kitchen and left them to break the ice—literally. "A glass of sherry? Wine?"

"A glass of sherry, please," Rachel requested because she'd read in books that's what real ladies ordered.

"I'll have a beer," Linc said.

A liquor tray was sitting on one of the tables, complete with decanters, glasses, and an ice bucket. But it included no beer, which Linc had already noted.

"Fix Rachel's drink. I know where the beer is kept." He crossed to the kitchen archway, leaving the two of them alone in the room.

After pouring the glass of sherry, Reece handed it to Rachel. His dark gaze probed her expression, but it was locked against him—as it always was.

"You have turned down all of my invitations to dinner. My niece must be more persuasive than I am," he murmured.

What could she say? That she had been wrong to accept this one? That would have been too rude. "She is a very lovely girl," Rachel said as if that explained it and sipped at the sherry.

Its dryness seemed to cake her tongue, leaving a strong after-taste. It had been a mistake to order it. She should have asked for something she knew she would like instead of attempting to impress Reece. She watched him splash whiskey into a tumbler of ice cubes and wished she could trade with him.

"Please sit down." He gestured toward the seat cushion of the sofa while he chose the armchair on its left. There was an aura of worldly authority about him that seemed so natural.

Rachel tried to emulate his aloof composure as she sank gracefully—or so she hoped—onto the couch. She couldn't help noticing how well the silk shirt fit the cut of his shoulders. He was so trim and manly that she couldn't look at him without feeling that wild fluttering in her stomach.

She had never believed such men truly existed, which was why she couldn't believe someone like Reece was really interested in her. For all intents and purposes, she had never been out of the Ozarks in her life except for that one trip to Chicago twenty years ago.

She took another sip of the sherry and almost couldn't swallow it. She tried to be very casual when she set the glass on the coffee table.

"Is the sherry too dry?" Reece inquired.

"It's fine," she lied.

Joanna was slipping a bibbed apron over her head when Linc walked into the kitchen. She glanced at him, sharply curious and suspicious. The lazy flick of his glance sent a rippling warning along her nerve ends. She felt raw and exposed, on edge in his presence.

"Do you want a beer?" he asked and walked straight to the refrigerator.

"No thanks." She tied the apron's bow at the back of her waist. The pop-top of an aluminum can sounded behind her as she turned on the burner under the pan of broccoli.

"Rachel made the dress she's wearing. You might want to compliment her on it," Linc suggested.

Joanna glanced to the side where he was standing, a hip leaning against the counter and a can of beer in his hand. His shirt was half-unbuttoned, showing more of his bronzed torso than she felt safe to see.

"I'll remember that," she said stiffly.

As she removed the potatoes from the oven, she switched the setting to broil for the trout. She was conscious of his eyes following her every move, tracking her like a cat sighting its prey.

"I never would have guessed you had domestic talents," Linc remarked.

"I had a very good teacher," she tried to keep the irritation out of her voice.

Tonight was too important for Reece. She didn't want to ruin it by losing her temper with Linc. It wouldn't be easy since he had the knack of rubbing her the wrong way. Completely unbidden, the thought came that he also knew how to rub her the right way; his kiss had been proof of that.

"Who? Your mother?"

"No—Reece. My mother has difficulty boiling water," Joanna admitted on a rebellious note.

Linc made no comment on that, as he straightened from the counter. "It's getting awfully quiet in the living room. I suggest you serve dinner as soon as possible. It might make up for the lack of conversation."

As he left the kitchen to rejoin the couple alone in the living room, Joanna conceded that he did have a point. Silence could become an insurmountable barrier. She remembered too well that Rachel had told her that she ran out of things to say after five minutes and Reece was showing no inclination to use his considerable charm to draw the woman into a conversation.

If that trend continued, it would be a long evening.

Removing the salad plates from the refrigerator, Joanna carried them out to the table. She glanced briefly into the living room where Linc seemed to be carrying the conversation. Her uncle didn't appear to be following the talk, his gaze continuously roaming over Rachel Parmelee who didn't look at him at all. When each of the place settings had a salad, Joanna slipped the broiler pan into the oven and took off her apron.

She entered the living room and paused near the table. "If you would come to the table, we can sit down for dinner." The seating arrangements were simple, the men and women sitting opposite each other. "That's a very lovely dress," she remarked and prompted her uncle, "Isn't it, Reece?"

"Yes, it is very lovely. Very becoming on you, Rachel," he agreed with a display of his old charm.

The compliment was rewarded by the softening of the woman's features and the sparkle that brightened her eyes. Joanna thought that at last they were getting somewhere.

"Did you make it yourself, Rachel?" she asked.

The widow lowered her gaze to the table as she picked up her salad fork. "Yes, I did."

Joanna interpreted the lowered eyes and quiet reply as a display of modesty. A knee nudged her right leg under the table. Since Linc was seated

117

on her right, it had to have been him. But she wasn't sure if it had been accidental or on purpose. Joanna slid him a glance and was confused by the hard look he was giving her.

Annoyed, she ignored him to concentrate on Rachel. "You certainly are an excellent seamstress. I wish you had time to give me some sewing lessons."

There was an uncomfortable silence for several seconds during which Joanna instinctively glanced at Linc. His mouth was pulled down at the corners in dry exasperation.

"Sewing is a matter of practice," Rachel replied at last. "A skill that is generally learned out of necessity."

"But once it is learned, it would be a shame not to use it," Reece inserted.

"Have you seen Jessie Bates lately?" Linc directed his question at Joanna, bringing about a complete change of topic.

"Not lately, no." She eyed him warily. "Why?"

"I thought he might have regaled you with more tales and superstitions of the Ozarks," he shrugged. "He is a walking encyclopedia of folklore."

"Well, he hasn't." Joanna was just as glad, too. She was still half convinced that she had made his superstition about the redbird flying across her path a self-fulfilling prophecy.

"I can remember one of my first meetings with Jessie," Reece recalled with a smile. "He explained to me about the 'law of the hills.'"

"What is the law of the hills?" Joanna was the

only one at the table who didn't smile at his comment.

"Ridgerunners—hill-folks—don't look favorably on the so-called outside authorities whether it's a sheriff, state, or federal agents. They prefer to handle their own problems," Linc explained. "It's commonly known as hill 'just-us.'"

At first, she thought he had said justice, then she caught his pun and smiled. "I won't ask how it works." She finished her salad and noticed that her uncle had also. "Excuse me while I check on the trout."

"Let me carry these plates out for you and help dish the food," Rachel volunteered as Joanna pushed her chair away from the table.

Before she stood up, she felt the toe of Linc's boot nudge her foot. She smothered the burst of irritation. She was well aware of how to act with guests. She certainly didn't need any sideline coaching from him.

"No, you stay here," Joanna refused the offer. "We didn't invite you here to put you to work. This is your day off."

With the salad plates stacked in her hand, she carried them to the kitchen and set them in the sink. It only took a few minutes to dish up the broccoli and arrange the broiled trout on a platter. This only left the baked potatoes and the cheese sauce. When they were served, she rejoined them at the table.

"This cheese sauce is delicious, Joanna. So smooth. Did you make it?" Rachel asked.

"Yes, but I can't take the credit. The recipe is a

family secret," she explained. "Actually I shouldn't say that because it belongs to Reece. He is a marvelous cook."

"I didn't know that." Rachel looked at him anew.

"Yes, I once considered training to be a master chef," he admitted and shrugged. "Now it is merely a hobby."

"With your hours, I doubt if you have much time to cook, do you, Rachel?" Joanna remarked sympathetically and was kicked in the shin by Linc. She breathed in sharply at the pain but he was already talking, covering her small sound.

"I don't know about you, Rachel, but I can fix a mean batch of scrambled egss," he declared, mocking their culinary feats.

"That's more in my line," Rachel admitted with a wan smile.

Through the rest of the main course and into dessert and coffee, the conversation vacillated over various subjects without ever becoming truly lively. On two other occasions, Joanna was prodded by Linc's foot. She no more understood the cause for it then than she did the other times.

Rachel finished her coffee and replaced the cup on its saucer. "I enjoyed the meal, Joanna, and I insist that you let me help with the clean-up."

"Sorry." Her smile was bright as she refused Rachel's offer again. "But Linc has already volunteered for kitchen duty tonight. This time you can relax after dinner and chat with Reece."

Joanna noticed how ill at ease the woman looked at the prospect, but it couldn't be helped. The object of this evening was to get the two together. Joanna carried some of the remaining dishes into the kitchen and Linc brought the rest.

"Did I *volunteer* to wash the dishes or dry them?" Linc mocked.

"Dry." The dishes clattered loudly as she stacked them in the sink with an impatient disregard for their breakability. "And would you mind explaining why you kept kicking me all night? It's a miracle I'm not limping."

"I was trying to keep you from putting your foot in your mouth, but I'm now convinced that's impossible," he said dryly.

"Why? What did I do?" Joanna stopped to stare at him incredulously.

"Do you want that answered point by point or just the highlights?" He lifted a dark brow in mocking inquiry.

"The highlights will do." She jammed the stopper in the sink drain and wished it was his face.

"A candlelight dinner isn't exactly subtle. You should have barbequed steaks outside so it could have been less formal and more relaxed. The only thing missing tonight was the violin music in the background."

"And?" She tightly prompted him to continue, irritated by the common sense of his answer.

"And—you should have complimented her on the dress and let it go at that. That's partly my fault since I told you she had made it herself. What I failed to mention was how self-conscious she felt because it didn't carry a fancy label, therefore it was unworthy and not up to Reece's standards."

"Now, that is ridiculous." She resented that attitude. "Reece isn't a snob."

"You know that, and I know that, but Rachel doesn't," Linc reasoned calmly as she turned on the taps to fill the sink with water.

Recognizing the inherent truth of his observation, Joanna sighed. "What else?"

"If you wanted her to feel comfortable, you should have allowed her to help serve. She isn't used to being waited on, not in this kind of situation," he stated.

"I wanted to show her that she was important, a guest," she defended her action.

"I'm not questioning your intentions, Joanna." There was a faint smile curving his mouth. "Unfortunately, you only succeeded in making her feel awkward."

"I see." The line of her mouth was tight. She pushed the faucet over to fill the other half of the double sink with rinse water. "Is there anything else?"

"Just one."

"That figures," she grumbled.

"If you wanted them to meet on common ground, they should be here in the kitchen doing the dishes instead of us. Maybe if Rachel saw Reece up to his elbows in dishsoap, she would realize he doesn't exist on some elevated plane," Linc concluded.

She attacked the dirty dishes, angry with herself for not seeing the things that had been so obvious to Linc. It didn't help that he had been the one to point out her shortcomings. That was salt on the wound.

"I have to admit," Linc went on as he lifted the dishes out of the rinse water and stacked them on the drainboard, "you do have a talent for saying and doing the wrong things at the wrong time."

"Thanks a lot," she murmured sarcastically. "I really needed that vote of confidence."

"I wouldn't worry about it." He began drying the dishes she washed. "After all, it's something they have to work out themselves. All you could have accomplished would have been to smooth the path a little but it's still up to them to walk down it."

"I suppose it is," Joanna sighed, but she did feel a little better.

He crooked a finger under her chin, startling her with his touch. Her widened gaze flew to his face, pleasantly rugged and lean. His mouth slanted in a half-smile. He rubbed a thumb over her cheek and explained, "You had some dishsoap on your face."

Unaware he'd already wiped it away, she lifted a wet hand to her cheek, trailing more soap bubbles across it. "Is it gone?"

He chuckled in his throat. "Not at that rate."

This time he used a corner of the dishtowel to wipe away the suds. "There. It's all gone."

Unexpectedly her gaze became locked by his. There was an uneven patter to her heartbeat, an unsteady rhythm to her breathing. A sudden, inexplicable tension knotted her stomach. She had an urge to smooth the springing thickness of his dark hair. With an effort, Joanna dragged her gaze away from him and tried to concentrate on the dirty dishes in the sink.

"Did any birds fly in front of you today?" Linc murmured the question.

She swallowed in an attempt to ease the sudden constriction in her throat. "No."

"That's funny."

At his cryptic reply, she glanced at him. Linc reached out and turned her away from the sink and into his arms, his mouth coming down to cover hers. Heat flared in her veins as she strained toward him, yet careful not to touch him with her wet hands. She pressed herself against the hard strength of his body.

His caressing hands became tangled in the ties of her apron. It brought them both back to the present. He released her slowly, breathing in deeply, a light continuing to smolder in his tawny eyes.

"You have to be the most exasperating female I've met," he said, the remark stinging her. "You get under a man's skin whether it's what he wants or not."

"Do you want me to get under your skin?"

Joanna didn't intend for her question to be as provocative as it sounded.

"Not as much as I want to get into yours," Linc replied with so much desire in his look that she had to turn back to the sink to quiet her own lusting thoughts.

Chapter Nine

The terrible pangs of self-consciousness returned in full force the minute Rachel left the dinner table and lost the buffer of Linc and Joanna. She was tongue-tied, helpless to find a subject to discuss with Reece. Her knees were weak as she walked to the couch where she had been sitting before dinner.

"Would you care for an after-dinner liqueur?" Reece paused in front of the fireplace. "Perhaps a brandy or Drambuie?"

"No, thank you." After the fiasco with the sherry, Rachel didn't intend to repeat the mistake by requesting something she had never tasted.

Then she noticed that Reece was turning away from the liquor tray to walk to the armchair he'd previously occupied on her right. She panicked a little when she thought he wasn't having a drink because she had refused one.

"Aren't you going to fix yourself something?" she asked.

"No, I don't care for alcohol that well," he explained and allowed a smile to pull at the corners of his mouth. "Except on occasions when I sometimes seek the dutch courage that's in the bottle."

It was difficult to imagine he would ever need that. He always seemed to be in command of any situation. Rachel wondered if he'd meant that because the remark implied he had needed the false courage of liquor before dinner. But she couldn't ask him about it.

"This cabin is very nice, isn't it?" She filled the silence with an empty remark and wished she had said something witty and intelligent.

"Yes," Reece agreed and looked around the room with quiet satisfaction. "I think of it as my second home. It is much more comfortable than my place in California. Sometimes I wish I could move the cabin there."

"It would be out of place." Just as she would be in Los Angeles. "Your home in California must be very grand."

Rachel could easily picture him in such a setting and was a little surprised to discover how well he blended into this rustic surrounding.

"It is quite large," he admitted then raised his downcast glance to look at her. "It is also quite empty."

"I'm sure you have many friends to fill it," she insisted.

There was a wry lift of his mouth. "A man in my position has a great many acquaintances, Rachel, but very few friends."

"I suppose." But she had difficulty believing that.

He seemed to sense it. "Are there not times when you are lonely?"

"Of course." She tried to make light of the admission with an indifferent smile but there were many times when loneliness weighed down her spirit.

"I used to think the night times were the worst," Reece mused. "Now I know it is the mornings—with no one sitting across the breakfast table and no one to wave goodbye to you when you leave for work."

There was a tight constriction in her chest at the apt way he described the emptiness that yawned at the start of each new day, with nothing to look forward to at the end of it except more of the same. Yet Rachel wasn't able to voice it as readily as he had. Her glance strayed to the window. Beyond its glass panes, crimson and gold banners were streaking the sky.

"Look at the sunset." She called Reece's attention to the window, relieved to change the subject. Rising from the couch, she walked to the window for a better view. "Isn't it beautiful?"

She marveled at the brilliant colors shading the clouds and coloring the hills. Hearing his approach, she glanced over her shoulder. He stopped behind her and a little to one side. The disturbing darkness of his gaze stayed on her for several seconds before swinging to the window.

"It is very beautiful," he agreed with a nod of his head.

His nearness started little tremors of excitement that she couldn't control. A strong sense of self-preservation insisted that she deny herself the pleasure she found in his company or suffer the consequences.

"I can't stay late," Rachel said and stared out the window.

Out of the corner of her eyes, she saw the sharp frown of displeasure Reece directed at her. She fought down the thrill that he didn't want her to leave yet.

"I have to be at the shop bright and early tomorrow morning," she justified her reason.

"You work too hard and too many hours," he criticized.

"It can't be helped," she shrugged.

"You should hire a qualified assistant who can operate the store in your absence so you can have more free time," Reece advised.

"That is easier said than done." Her sidelong glance was both amused and resigned to the situation.

"Do you know why I say that?" The lilting inflection of his voice put a question mark at the end of the sentence. "There is so little time left. I want to spend every possible minute that I can with you. I am selfish. I want you to have more free hours so you can be with me."

She was thrown by the vibrating pitch of his voice that spoke with such intensity. It left her shaken and unnerved, unable to combat this undermining of her defenses.

"It . . . isn't possible." She faltered over her reply.

"When will I see you again?" When his direct question was met with silence, a smile twisted his mouth. "Or should I have Joanna ask that question for me? She seems to be more successful at obtaining an affirmative reply than I am. I shall have to learn her secret."

"There isn't any secret." Rachel assured him quickly. "It just worked out this way. Summer is my busy season and I—" She had used the shop as an excuse so many times that it sounded tired even to her. She abandoned it altogether. "There are dozens of ladies who would be more than delighted to spend time with you."

"It wouldn't matter if there were a million," Reece declared as he turned to face her. The warm firm touch of his hands catapulted her heart into her throat. "It is still *you* I'm asking, Rachel. Linc argues that I must be patient because you don't know me, but how patient must I be? Ask me what it is you want to know and I'll tell you. I want to be with *you*, Rachel, and I think—" He paused to lightly cup her cheek in his hand and tilt her face up. Although she tried, she couldn't resist the magnetic force of his charm and felt all her carefully guarded defenses melt away under his possessive look. "—you want to be with me."

Rachel couldn't say it. "Yes, but—" There were too many differences, too many obstacles.

"Sssh." He pressed his thumb to her lips before she could add more. "For now, it is enough that you have said 'yes' to me." She was incapable of arguing the point. "You close your shop early on Sunday, don't you? You don't keep it open in the evenings?"

"I generally close around six," she admitted.

"Then I will pick you up at six. Bring some old clothes and we'll go fishing," Reece stated.

"Fishing?" It was the last thing Rachel had expected him to suggest. A movie, dinner, a show perhaps—but not fishing. She couldn't keep the stunned reaction out of her expression.

"Yes, fishing." He frowned at her failure to endorse his suggestion. "Don't you like to fish? I thought you might enjoy the chance to be outside. You spend so much of your time indoors."

"I like to fish," she assured him, then qualified the answer, "At least I did. It's been years since I went fishing."

"Would you like to go Sunday?" This time he asked.

"Yes." It sounded novel and fun. "I'll have to get a license," she remembered.

"That's easily handled," Reece said and began to outline his plans for the evening. "I'll pick you up at six and get your license. We'll fish until dark and cook whatever we catch for a late supper."

"What if we don't catch anything?" She raised the possibility, not fully aware how easily she was joking with him, how naturally she was reacting.

"Then we will come back here and you can scramble me some eggs. And I will love it." His light tone became progressively serious until he ended on a husky note.

Under the burning darkness of his gaze, she stopped breathing. Her senses quivered in anticipation as his hand tightened on her shoulder, impelling her forward. His kiss was warm and firm, his needs controlled. It was all too brief to satisfy either of them, but it held an exciting promise that quickened her blood.

"I'll drive you home," Reece stated.

Rachel nodded, then remembered belatedly, "Linc—"

"Wait here," he interrupted, "and I'll tell them we're going."

"Okay," she smiled a contented agreement and watched him cross the room to the kitchen.

She felt as giddy and gay as a teenager who had just accepted an invitation from a boy she'd had a crush on for years. It was a sensation a mature forty-year-old woman didn't expect to experience again.

When Reece entered the kitchen, there weren't any more dirty dishes to be washed. Linc was drying the last pan while Joanna wiped off the range top.

Linc glanced over his shoulder. "If you've come to see if we need any help, Reece, your timing is excellent. We have just finished the dishes."

Reece's laugh drew Joanna's gaze. He was practically beaming. "No, I came to tell you that I'm driving Rachel home," he explained the reason for his presence. "She has to work tomorrow."

"Are you leaving now?" Joanna wondered.

"Yes. I'll be back later," her uncle promised and retraced his steps to the living room.

Joanna stared thoughtfully at the archway where he had disappeared while she folded the wet dishcloth and draped it over the sink divider. Linc was hanging up his towel on the rack. She cast him a sideways glance.

"It seems the dinner was a success after all," she murmured and reached behind her back to untie the apron bow. When she pulled the tie, it knotted. "Damn," she swore softly and struggled with the knot before giving up. "Will you untie this for me, Linc?" she demanded in irritation. "I can't see what I'm doing."

"Sure." He came up behind her.

Joanna faced the sink, her hands resting on the counter so they wouldn't be in his way. As he worked to free the knot, the touch of his hands along the small of her back caused a disturbing sensation that tingled up her spine. She heard her uncle's car drive out of the yard.

"Haven't you got it untied yet?" she demanded impatiently.

"Patience," he counseled. "By the way, the dinner was very good tonight. With a little practice, you might make some man a good wife."

"With a little more practice, you could become

a good wife, too," Joanna retorted, twisting and throwing back his sexist remark.

The knot was freed, loosening the apron around her waist. She slipped the haltered neckline over her head and stopped in the middle of folding the apron as his hands settled on her shoulders, rubbing them in an intimate fashion.

"You could have beautiful shoulders if you didn't carry that big chip on them all the time," Linc commented.

"If it wasn't for men like you, it wouldn't be there." She twisted away from his hands with a shrugging turn of her shoulders and moved a pace away. She could feel his narrowed gaze.

"You like being a deliberately aggravating female, don't you?" Linc challenged.

She gave him a wide-eyed look of mock innocence. "Because I make you itch?"

"I've decided it's a heat rash. Nothing a cold shower won't cure." The natural curve of his mouth deepened with dryness as topaz lights glittered in his brown eyes.

The double meaning wasn't lost on her. Heat warmed her cheeks, but she didn't know if it was caused by his insinuation of sex or his off-hand dismissal that she could arouse any lasting passion. She glared at him silently.

A satisfied smile spread slowly across his expression. "This is the first time I've ever seen you at a loss for words—especially sharp ones. Maybe there's hope for you yet," Linc suggested.

"Very funny." She found her sarcasm.

"The battle of the sexes is usually fought with words. Didn't you know that?" he mocked.

"Who said I was fighting?" Joanna challenged.

"You are. Do you know why?" he asked.

"You seem to know everything. Why don't you tell me?" Her jaw was tightly clenched.

"You don't respect anyone you can push around. By the same token, every time you're pushed, you push back. Somewhere, sometime, you're going to have to work out a compromise," Linc advised.

There was the sting of tears at the back of her eyes, but she kept her head held high and proud and showed no expression. A weariness passed over his face and he turned from her.

"Thanks for dinner," he said. "Tell Reece I'll see him."

Joanna stared as he walked out of the kitchen, shocked that he was actually leaving. She realized she didn't want him to go. She took a step after him and heard the front door slam. Halting, she listened and heard the start of a car's engine. When its roar faded into the night, there was only silence in the cabin, a silence broken by the ticking of the clock.

Chapter Ten

$\mathcal{I}$t was well over an hour before Reece returned from driving Rachel Parmelee home. When he walked in the door, his dark eyes shining and his handsome features radiating an inner happiness, Joanna felt a twinge of envy.

"You certainly took Rachel on the long way home," she observed with a glance at the clock, teasing him with her smile.

"We began talking and lost track of time." Reece was in too good a mood to take offense at her affectionate ribbing.

"Talking, huh?" Joanna moved closer and inspected the pink smudge on his white collar. "Is that how this lipstick got on your shirt?"

He glanced down, briefly self-conscious, then

laughed in his throat. The sound held a note of triumph, a battle long-fought and finally won.

"There are other, equally satisfactory methods of communication besides talking, as you already know," he stated.

She was pleased to see him so happy and contented. "When are you seeing her again?"

"Sunday," Reece answered without hesitation. "We're going fishing together."

"Fishing?" Joanna showed her surprise at his questionable choice for a romantic outing.

"That's exactly what Rachel said." A tiny crease showed on his forehead.

"I can understand why," Joanna replied. "Going fishing isn't exactly a romantic thing to do." Then she remembered Linc had indicated Rachel was uncomfortable with a staged, romantic setting. She quickly changed her opinion of his plans. "But I think it's a great idea. It's much easier for a person to relax and be themselves when they're fishing."

Her explanation erased his last doubts and he turned his mind to other things. "When did Linc leave?"

"Shortly after you did," she admitted and felt the quiet scrutiny of his eyes.

"I thought he would stay later than that," he remarked.

Joanna shrugged her lack of an explanation for his decision, uncomfortable with the subject. She went back to one that was safer. "Do you want me to make myself scarce Sunday night?"

"It isn't necessary as far as I'm concerned," he assured her. "Naturally you are free to make whatever plans you wish."

Late on Sunday afternoon, Reece was preparing to leave the cabin to pick up Rachel. Joanna was curled up in an armchair with a book that she pretended to be interested in, because she didn't want Reece to think she was at loose ends for something to do. The telephone rang. She started to uncoil her legs to answer it but he waved her back into the chair.

"I'll answer it." He walked to the phone and picked up the receiver. "Reece Morgan speaking."

Absently curious, Joanna watched recognition register in his expression as the caller obviously identified himself as someone her uncle knew. Then Reece was glancing her way.

"Yes, she's here. Just a minute." His hand covered the mouthpiece. "It's Linc. He wants to speak to you."

Surprise flickered across her face. Her heartbeat quickened as she pushed out of the chair and crossed the room to take the receiver from her uncle's hand. A little nervous, she took the phone and lifted it to her ear.

"Hello?"

"Joanna." Linc's voice quietly drawled her name in greeting. "Do you know how to ride a horse?"

She was too startled by the question to do more than give a simple answer. "Yes."

"Change into some jeans and we'll go riding," he instructed.

"When?" she asked blankly.

"Now. It'll probably take me about twenty minutes to ride down to the cabin. Can you be ready by then?"

"Yes." It wouldn't take that long to change clothes.

"Okay, I'll see you then."

There was a click and the buzz of a dial tone in her ear. She kept the phone in her hand an instant longer then hung it up. When she looked up, Reece was watching her with a bemused look.

"That was a very brief conversation," he remarked.

"Linc's coming down," she explained the reason for his call. "We're going horseback riding." Suddenly realizing her twenty minutes was being used up, she moved toward the stairs. "I have to change yet."

"I'll be leaving. Have a good time." He raised a hand in farewell as he retreated toward the door.

As she raced up the stairs, Joanna heard the car pulling out of the drive. Changing out of her shorts and suntop, she tugged on a pair of brushed denims and a pin-striped blouse. After running a brush through her ash-blonde hair, she dabbed on some lipgloss. Since she didn't have a pair of riding boots with her, she slipped on a pair of canvas sneakers and tied the laces.

She had barely reached the bottom of the

stairs when she heard the clip-clopping of horses' hooves out on the road, followed by the rolling snort of a horse. As she crossed the living room to the front door, she could see Linc riding into the driveway astride a dappled buckskin and leading a saddled, blaze-faced bay. By the time she reached the door and had walked outside, he had halted the horses.

Joanna paused a little uncertainly. "Hello," she said. After the way he had left so abruptly the other night, she didn't know what his attitude would be toward her now.

"Hello, yourself." His smile was lazy as his glance ran over her in quiet approval.

"Are we ready?" Relief relaxed her features into a bright smile.

The saddle groaned as he leaned forward to pass her the reins of the second horse. "Do you need some help mounting?" The brim of his western hat shadowed his eyes, but she was conscious of their warmth and interest.

"I think I can manage." She looped the reins over the horse's neck as Linc maneuvered his horse out of her way.

It was a long stretch to the stirrup. Joanna had to hop a couple of times to keep her balance before she got a toe in it. Gripping the saddle-horn, she swung into the seat. She adjusted the length of the reins in her hand, aware of the swiveling ears of her alert mount. She patted its sleek neck and crooned a few words to the horse so it would know her voice.

"All set?" Linc asked.

She gave an affirmative nod. "Where are we going?"

A touch of the rein turned her horse alongside of his buckskin. Both animals moved out at a walk, eager yet obedient.

"I thought we'd ride over to Jessie's and cut through his place to the lake," Linc answered. "Is that all right with you?"

Joanna darted a quick look at him to see if he was mocking her, but the expression on his rugged features was bland. "That's fine." She let her attention swing back to her horse and the road ahead.

"You're not a bad rider," he observed.

There was an impulse to make a quick retort at the back-handed compliment, but Joanna smothered it. "It's a good horse."

"Coffee is my sister's favorite. She used to ride him all the time."

She noticed the way the horse's ears pricked at the mention of its name. "Coffee. Is that what they call you, fella?" Joanna murmured to it, then glanced self-consciously at Linc who didn't seem to find anything wrong with talking to the horse. "Doesn't your sister ride her anymore?"

"Not since she got married and moved to her own home," he replied.

"Oh." She fell silent, listening to the steady clop of hooves, the jingle of bridle chains, and squeaking leather. "Why haven't you gotten married?"

"Too busy, I guess." He shifted in the saddle, his head lifted as he idly looked around.

"Do you mean you're not a confirmed bachelor?" she teased.

"Nope." Again there was a dry and lazy smile. "How about you?"

"I'm not sure that I want to get married," Joanna admitted, unexpectedly serious. A wry grimace tugged at her expression. "I haven't seen many 'happy' marriages in California. Of course, I look at Reece and then I want to believe—for his sake."

"Rachel?"

"Yes. I've never seen him so relaxed and carefree. He's practically walking on air." She smiled. "He's seeing her tonight. They're going fishing—of all things." Her side glance caught his look. "I know," she nodded. "They'll meet on the same level."

"You are quite a contradiction, Joanna." He shook his head in mild amazement. "Here you are match-making, yet you claim not to believe in the 'happily ever after' part."

"It doesn't make sense, does it?" she admitted with a faint laugh.

"No," he agreed and kneed his horse into a reaching trot.

Joanna urged her mount to keep pace. The jarring gait eliminated more conversation as they followed the rough and twisting road. The heat of the afternoon was fading, the sun's rays slanted against the earth. The shadows cast by the trees were lengthened across the road. Joanna turned her face to the cooling breeze their pace generated.

Where the road smoothed out, Linc spurred his horse into a rocking lope and Joanna followed suit. They stayed in a slow canter until they neared the turn-off to Jessie Bates's cabin. Checking their horses to a blowing walk, they turned down the narrow lane and followed it back to the log cabin. A mule brayed, announcing their arrival. Her horse snorted and turned its head to study its hybrid cousin.

"Hello! Anybody home!" Linc called.

There was a stirring inside the cabin. The hinges on the screen door squealed a protest as the door was pushed open and Jessie stepped out, yawning and scratching his head, ruffling hair that was already rumpled.

"Ya' caught me nappin'," he said and blinked his eyes. "What d'ya want?"

"We thought we'd ride down to the lake," Linc explained.

"Oh," Jessie grunted. "I thought ya mighta come to visit."

Joanna caught the trace of disappointment in his voice and glanced at Linc. He'd heard it, too, and lifted an eyebrow in silent question. She answered with a slight nod.

"We did," she told Jessie and kicked her foot out of the off-stirrup to dismount. "Unless you have other plans, of course."

"None at all," he said, brightening a little.

Linc had stepped to the ground and reached to take the reins of her horse so he could tie them both to the corral post. "What have you been up to, Jess?"

"Nothin'." He shook his head. "You know that's a real problem, too."

"Why?" Joanna frowned in concern.

"'Cause if a fella's doin' nothin', how can he stop to rest?" His hands were outstretched, palm upward, in a beseeching gesture.

It took a second for his witticism to register, then she laughed. "Jessie, I'm never sure when you're serious or pulling my leg."

He recoiled in mock offense. "I'm serious. It is a problem." But she could see the laughing twinkle in his eye.

"Let me know when you come up with a solution." She walked to the porch where he was standing. Linc's angle intercepted her path as she reached her destination.

"Grab a step and sit yourself down." Jessie waved a hand to the porch steps. He claimed the top one while Joanna and Linc sat down on the second. "Going ridin', eh?"

"Yes, it should be a pleasant evening for it," Linc replied, tipping his hat to the back of his head.

"If'n I was you, I'd make a point of gettin' back afore dark," he nodded sagely.

"Why?" Joanna shifted her position to sit sideways on the step so she could see the slightly eccentric character.

"It's a night for 'haints.'"

"Haints? What is that?" She'd never heard the word.

"Haunts. Ghosts," Linc translated.

Her leg was being pulled again, she realized. "You aren't trying to tell me that you believe in ghosts?" she laughed uncertainly.

"Ain't sayin' I do, an' I ain't sayin' I don't," Jessie hedged. "But thare's folks that claim to have seen some things that would stand your hair on end."

Joanna couldn't help being skeptical. "Such as?"

"Have ya' ever heard tell of Breadtray Mountain?" he challenged.

"No." She shook her head and glanced at Linc. He was lighting a cigarette, his hand cupping the flame. She couldn't see his face. "What about it?"

"It's a mountain over in Stone County. There's been a lot of stories told about that place but one thing is a fact—hill-folks don't go around there after dark."

"Why not?"

"It's haunted, that's why not." He gave her a look that questioned her intelligence for asking such a thing.

"How do you know it's haunted?" Joanna persisted.

"I never said *I* knew it. I'm just tellin' you what I've heard," he explained patiently, neither claiming to believe it or disbelieve it. "The stories say that Spaniards buried a bunch of gold there years ago. Right after that, they was attacked by Indians and all of 'em were killed. If you go to Breadtray Mountain at night, you can hear the sobs and screams of those dying men." His voice became low and theatrical as he bent closer to Joanna, his eyes widening.

Despite her common sense, she felt a little shiver run down her spine. "Why would they want to haunt the mountain?"

"Some say them ghosts will stay 'til somebody finds that gold they buried. Those Spanish soldiers can't rest 'til it's dug up and recovered."

"And nobody's found it?" She already guessed the answer.

"Nope." He shook his head sadly. "Tho' plenty a'people has looked."

"There probably isn't any gold or any ghosts," Joanna doubted.

"I s'pose you don't believe in ghosts just 'cause you've never seen one," Jessie challenged. All the while, Linc sat quietly smoking his cigarette and watching the two of them with indulgent interest. "Just 'cause you ain't seen one, don't mean there ain't none."

"I know it doesn't, but—"

"Ghosts are spirits. Most of the time, they're invisible. But there is a way you can see 'em," he declared.

"How?"

"A rider can see a ghost—even if it's invisible —by looking at it from behind his horse's ears," Jessie stated with complete certainty. "Jest sight down that horse's nose like it was a rifle."

"What!" Joanna exclaimed in disbelief at the wild claim.

"Why's that so hard to believe?" Jessie protested. "Animals—horses and dogs—can see things we can't. If there's a ghost around, your horse will be pointing his head at it. Why do you think folks say that a horse 'spooks' when he shies from somethin' that his rider can't see. You try it sometime. Just look between his ears when you're sittin' a'straddle him."

"I'll do it," she stated to put an end to all this superstitious nonsense.

"You wouldn't happen to have a pitcher of that cold spring water in the house, Jessie? I'm a little thirsty," Linc said. "How about you, Joanna?"

"If you have some, yes," she nodded, remembering that he didn't have running water in the old cabin.

"It'll just take me a minute to fetch it." He rose with a turn and walked into the house.

Joanna looked at Linc and lowered her voice. "Does he really believe all that nonsense about the ghosts?"

"You should be here when he really gets wound up. Of course, it's best when it's dark and you're sitting around the flickering light of a campfire. He can scare you silly with some of his tales." Linc paused. "Storytelling is almost a lost art. Radio, television, movies, they have taken it over."

"I guess that's true," Joanna agreed.

When Jessie returned, he was carrying two mismatched glasses of water. It was cool and sweet. She drank every drop of hers. Jessie nodded his approval.

"Best water around," he stated with pride.

"Mmm, delicious." She wiped a droplet of water from her chin and handed him back the glass. "Thanks."

"Ready to start out?" Linc asked and pushed to his feet.

"Sure." She stood to walk with him to the horses.

"Keep an eye out for them haints," Jessie advised.

Chapter Eleven

The boat was a simple runabout, powered by an outboard motor. A pair of flotation cushions offered some relief from the hardness of the board seats. Any change of position in the small boat almost required logistic planning even though there were only two people. With all their fishing paraphernalia—tacklebox, bait, nets, and rods—there wasn't much room for their feet.

In a quiet cove, the boat drifted on the still waters of the lake. The skeletons of trees poked their white limbs above the surface close to shore, long ago drowned by the damming of White River that had formed the lake.

The striated layers of a limestone bluff were drenched by the rays of the setting sun. Hugging the shoreline, a mallard hen kept counting heads and quacking to make sure her brood of ducklings stayed together. High overhead, a hawk soared in a lazy circle, gliding effortlessly on the air currents.

The boat rocked gently as Rachel shifted her position slightly and cast her line into the deep water. Her first few attempts had been uncoordinated and inaccurate, but she had since regained the knack of casting so the line sailed out smoothly and on target.

"Very good," Reece nodded in smiling approval.

His dark eyes noticed the way she beamed proudly at his compliment. They noticed a lot of things about her, from her appearance to the unmasking of her personality. A cloth hat covered her light brown hair, its shapeless brim protecting her pale complexion from the burning rays of the sun.

Over a modest tanktop of yellow knit she was wearing an old blue blouse with long sleeves as a light jacket. At Reece's insistence, there was a life belt around her trim waist. Splotches of white paint on her faded jeans indicated they had long ago been relegated to less than everyday clothes. The worn material softly hugged her hips and legs in a way that was decidedly attractive.

Dressed as she was, there was a gamin charm about her. A complete abandonment of pretence that she was any more than what he saw. Proud, spirited . . . vulnerable, she was naturally woman. Her eyes no longer tried to keep him from seeing inside.

Rachel was all the things he had thought her to be and more, much more. A heady excitement swelled inside him until he wanted to shout his happiness to the world.

"What are you smiling about?" Rachel studied him with a look that was wary yet openly warm.

"You." His smile deepened with incredible inner pleasure.

"I must look a mess," she admitted without embarrassment.

"A beautiful mess," Reece corrected in a vibrant tone of undisguised adoration.

Her attention shifted to her fishing rod as she tested the tautness of the line. "One of the first signs of age is failing eyesight. I think you need yours tested." She was deliberately provocative.

With a small, negative movement of his head, Reece dismissed her reasoning. "I have contracted a malady that attacks all ages," he explained. "It is a widely known fact that love is blind."

Rachel faltered, unable to look at him, afraid to breathe, afraid to hope that it wasn't an empty phrase. Her fingers closed tightly around the handle of the fishing rod. For several seconds, there was only the quiet lapping of the water against the sides of the boat.

"I promised myself I wouldn't rush you." His sigh was heavy with irritation. "That I would wait until—" He stopped in midsentence then abruptly refused to retract his admission. "Love is a beautiful word. It is what I feel, and I don't regret saying it."

When she finally looked at him, she was fighting the happiness that misted his image. "Do you know what I feel like right now, Reece?" Her voice was husky with emotion. "I can't seem to act my age. My legs are like rubber and, I swear, I'd swoon if you touched me."

The grimness was erased from his expression as he leaned forward, absently setting his pole aside. His eyes were dark with longing, possessive in their study of her face. He brought up his hand to caress her cheek. There was a fluttering of her lashes but she didn't swoon.

"It isn't too soon?" He needed to verify that she didn't object to this quantum leap in their relationship.

"It probably is," she replied. "There hasn't been enough time to be sure. It could all be a mistake."

"It isn't. Don't ask me how I know but it isn't," he insisted. "We are not young any more, Rachel, and I'm glad. We have the experience to see and appreciate the worth of what we share, and the wisdom to treasure it."

The smallest smile touched her mouth. "You sound so wise and experienced. You must be a lot older than I am, because there isn't a single sane or sensible thought in my head," she declared with the faintest trace of humor.

His soft laugh was barely audible. The warmth of his breath caressed her skin as he brought his mouth against her lips. They strained toward each other across the distance between their seats, bridging it with their kiss yet unable to close the gap.

The kiss burned with the passion of the young, its fire sealing the promises of their words. There was a certain savoring quality about the embrace, a sense of rapturous wonder that must be tasted slowly to be enjoyed.

When the feast was brought to a reluctant end, Rachel sighed in partial satisfaction. They continued to gaze at one another as if assuring themselves that it all was real, and their contentment was mutual.

A passing speedboat sent its wake into the cove where the runabout bobbed on its rippling waves. Reece let his gaze slide to their surroundings and return to her.

"Here we are in a small boat in the middle of the lake with smelly fish bait at our feet." There was regret in his bemused expression. "It is hardly a romantic setting. I can't even properly hold you in my arms. Shall we go back to the cabin?"

She straightened to sit erectly, mocking him with a reproving look. "Without catching our supper?" she chided. "I don't know about you, but I'd like something more substantial than scrambled eggs."

Reece chuckled. "It is amazing how hungry I suddenly feel."

The reel began to spin on Rachel's rod as a fish

took the baited hook on her line. The sudden sound startled her until she realized what it was.

Then she cried out in triumph, "I've got one!"

Her fingers became all thumbs as she clumsily began to reel it in. Reece laughed heartily at her uncoordinated efforts.

"It's probably a minnow," he teased.

"That's more than you've caught," she responded to his challenging remark. Just at that second, the fish broke the surface of the water. Rachel stared at the size of it and forgot to keep reeling in the line. "Did you see that?"

Reece was already whistling in surprise. "It's a big one. Don't lose it." He reached for her pole. "You'd better let me land it."

"Oh, no." She moved the pole out of his reach. "This one's mine. I'm not going to let you take credit for catching it."

His glance of surprise became one of approval. He liked the spark of competition in her eyes and that assertion of self-reliance. He sat back and let his help take the form of encouragement and advice.

A worn trail wandered away from Jessie's cabin and eventually wound its way to the lake. The way was narrow and they were forced to ride single file with Linc taking the lead astride the dappled buckskin. When they reached the shore, the forest gave way to a natural clearing and Joanna urged her horse to ride up alongside of the buckskin.

"Where do you suppose Reece took Rachel

fishing?" She could see several boats out on the lake but they were all too far away.

"It's hard to tell. It's a big lake," Linc didn't hazard a guess.

Something rustled in the brush near the edge of the trees. Her horse turned its head toward the area, snorting and pricking its ears. Joanna looked, too, but saw nothing.

"Aren't you going to test out Jessie's theory?" Linc asked with an amused, sideways glance.

She reddened slightly, because it had been on her mind to lean forward in the saddle so she could look between her horse's ears and possibly sight a spectre.

"There are no such things as ghosts," she stated emphatically and settled deeper in the saddle seat.

"But you were going to look, weren't you?" he guessed.

She started to vigorously deny it but the laughter in his eyes was completely without malice. A slightly sheepish look crossed her face.

"For a split second, I was," Joanna admitted. "I really don't know why. I don't believe for a minute that I would see anything."

"But, just in case—" Linc added the qualification that had prompted her initial reaction.

"Yes, just in case," she agreed on a note of amused self-derision.

"You're not alone. Everyone who has ever heard that story has tested it out to see if it's true. It's human nature to be curious and skeptical at the same time," he grinned, then changed the subject to point to the top of the hill. "There's a great view from that knob. Do you want to ride up and take a look?"

"Sure."

This time there was no trail to follow and Linc had to blaze a new path. It was long and twisting, dictated by the course of least resistance. Even then, Joanna still found herself dodging and ducking low-hanging tree limbs. Occasionally their progress was punctuated by the strike of metal against stone as the shod horses scrambled over rocky stretches.

As they neared the top of the hill, the ground became barren of trees and undergrowth. The slope became steep and the horses lunged the last few feet to the crest. Joanna reined in her horse beside Linc's and let it blow.

He stepped out of his saddle in a single, coordinated move and held the bridle of her horse while she dismounted to join him on the ground. The muscles in her legs quivered slightly, showing the strain of the ride.

"I have the feeling I'm going to be stiff tomorrow," she said.

"A long soak in the tub tonight should ease most of the soreness." Linc released the reins to both bridles, letting the ends trail loose.

The horses were trained to stand when the reins dragged the ground. They lowered their heads to graze on the tufts of sun-yellowed grass on the knoll.

His hand rested on her shoulder near the base of her neck, its slight pressure guiding her away from the horses. Joanna took her first look at the panoramic view from the high knob. The western horizon was turning yellow as the fiery gold orb of the sun sank lower in the sky. In all directions, there was the roll of high-ridged hills that seemed without end, their slopes thick with trees. The vantage point gave her a view of the many-armed lake, its surface shimmering like glass.

"I promised you a view," Linc said.

Joanna realized they had stopped. "You were right." It was an understatement but there weren't any words to do it justice.

"The Ozark Mountains are one of the oldest mountain ranges in the country, possibly the world. You're looking at what is probably the last hardwood forest we have," he explained.

She became conscious of the weight of his hand on her shoulder and the touch of his fingers against the sensitive skin on her neck. Through her clothes, she could feel the warmth of his body heat as he stood close beside her. It rippled through her like the spreading heat of a warm fire.

"The mountain men trapped their furs here and the Indians hunted the game of the forests, but this area wasn't really settled until the start of the nineteenth century. Most of the early pioneers came from the Southern Appalachians. They brought with them their stories, superstitions, and sure-cure remedies. The very roughness of the land isolated them from the rest of the world and gave birth to their culture."

"Where did they learn all their superstitions?" Joanna wondered. "From the Indian? The Negro?"

"As I said, they came from the Appalachians, which was settled mainly by the English. I guess there are areas where even the accent is decidedly English. So are the songs and stories."

"And the English claim to have an abundance of ghosts haunting their many castles," she remembered. A scattering of clouds were turning orange as the sun began to settle behind them. "Look at the sunset," she murmured.

"Let's settle back and watch it," Linc stated and pressed his hand on her shoulder to push her to the ground.

While she sat cross-legged, Linc stretched out on his side, propping himself up with an elbow. He tore off a long blade of grass and chewed on one end. The cloud-haze turned the sun into a crimson red ball that spread its stain across the sky. Joanna watched the hues change from gold to coral and red.

"People aren't going to believe me about this place," she declared.

"Why?"

"Back in California, they will laugh when I tell them about nearly running into a wagon pulled by a team of mules. They'll think I made it up. You have to admit it does sound farfetched," she pointed out with a wry shake of her head. "Then there's Jessie."

"He does have to be seen to be believed," Linc agreed.

"They'd think I was crazy if I told them how Jessie predicted I would be kissed twice before nightfall just because that cardinal flew across my path. And the ghost stories, and looking between a horse's ears to see one." It stretched the imagination too far.

"And how will you describe me to your friends?" He watched while he twirled the blade of grass between his fingers.

"You?" Joanna repeated, momentarily at a loss for a reply. "Oh, well"—she stalled—"that's easy. I'll just describe this bossy man, always throwing his weight around and telling people how to behave. You are the only blight on an otherwise perfect vacation." She deliberately baited him.

"Is that a fact?" Linc rose to the challenge.

With a laugh, Joanna attempted to elude his reaching hand, but he caught the loose fold of her blouse near the waist. It checked her escape long enough for him to grab an arm with his other hand. Her laughing shriek didn't faze him as he dragged her backward onto the ground.

She struggled briefly, trying to get free, but his superior strength was too much for her. She stopped fighting him and lay passively under his grip, her head resting on the ground while silent laughter dominated her expression. She looked up at him, out of breath.

"I was only kidding," she insisted, unable to sound totally serious. "I'm sorry, really."

"How sorry?" Linc demanded.

Something in the tawny gleam of his eyes

changed the mood from playful to one that was filled with a sexual tension. Her heart hammered wildly against her ribs as she felt the weight of his body pressing down on hers, holding her to the ground.

His hands pinned her wrists and his face was inches above hers. There was a raw ache inside her that seemed to spring from nowhere. Her gaze strayed to his mouth, its firm, well-cut line hovering above her.

"Linc," she murmured in unconscious longing.

He lowered his mouth onto hers in hard possession and all of her resistance went up in flames. Her lips parted as he kissed her deeply. She wasn't conscious of slipping her hands free of his grip, but somehow she had managed it because her fingers were threading through the springing thickness of his hair, rough and sensual against her palms.

She felt light and boneless, putty in his hands, hands that were caressing her with a sureness and ease. It was all very earthy and natural. When his fingers tugged her blouse free from the waistband of her jeans, it seemed right. Her nerve ends thrilled at the touch of his hand against her flesh, so warm and gently evocative, arousing and exploring.

She seemed filled with the golden fire of sundown, all radiant and glowing. It was a wild, new sensation that hinted at something greater. Needles of sexual excitement pierced her, stabbing at her loins with the need to know that fulfillment.

When he pulled his mouth from hers, it was to explore the curve of her throat and descend to the high, warm swell of her breasts. The front of her blouse was opened to expose the creamy gold flesh of her braless torso.

Delicious shudders quivered through her when Linc mouthed the taut peak of her breast. His hands were stroking down her body, inviting the rhythmic movement of her hips against them. Their caress offered a vague satisfaction but not the complete kind that Joanna desired.

Her fingers tightened in the virile thickness of his hair, applying pressure in an attempt to express the urgent needs of her flesh. Tiny sounds were coming from her throat, sounds that Joanna wasn't conscious of making. His body weight shifted as he raised his head as if he intended to withdraw.

"Please." Her voice wavered above a whisper, wanting him in the rawest sense. "Don't stop now, Linc." She was practically begging him to make love to her but she didn't care.

The dark blaze of the setting sun cast a burnished light on his stark, powerful features. They held only one expression, the same one she was feeling.

"Why?" He wanted her to verbalize her reason, to admit to the passion consuming her bones.

But that required an honest examination of

her emotions. All she wanted was to enjoy these sensations. Words seemed totally unnecessary at a time like this. A much more satisfactory communication could be achieved through physical expression.

"What difference does it make?" Her fingers linked together behind his neck to pull him down to her once more. "Just let it be something to tell my friends."

She closed her eyes in anticipation when Linc started to give in to the pressure of her hands. A second later, his fingers were gripping her wrists and pulling her arms from around his neck. In dazed confusion, she opened her eyes and blinked at the harshness of his features.

As he stood up, Linc pulled her to her feet. Joanna staggered against him, her sense of balance slow to return. There was a controlled roughness to his touch when he steadied her.

"What is it?" She didn't understand what was the matter with him. Why was he so angry?

"The sun's almost down. We have to start back or else we'll be riding in the dark." He let go of her and covered the distance to the horses with long, impatient strides.

Joanna followed him, stumbling as she tried to hurry. While part of her mind conceded that there was a legitimacy to the reason he'd given her, she knew instinctively that it wasn't the real one. When she reached him, he had gathered the reins to both horses.

"What did I do wrong, Linc?" Joanna persisted in her determined search for an explanation.

"Do I have to spell it out for you?" His mouth was grim. "You'd like to go back to that patch of grass and finish what we started, wouldn't you?" Her cheeks reddened at his bluntness. It sounded so crude and animalistic put that way. "Well, I don't," he snapped.

"Why?" She was stung into challenging him. "You seemed anxious enough a few minutes ago."

"Maybe I just don't like the idea of being a vacation fling—someone to brag to your friends about back in California." He threw the words in her face.

"As if *you* wouldn't brag about it to *your* friends," Joanna retorted with sarcasm. "Or are you a saint?"

"I'm no saint." There was a flatness to his voice as Linc worked to bring his anger under control—and succeeded. "Indiscriminate sex was all right when I was young and wild. If the girl was willing, so was I." In the slight pause, his gaze raked her. "Now I want her to be ready, too."

"What makes you think I was willing?" Joanna thoughtlessly snapped at his presumptive statement.

His look became dry and mocking. "You were the one who said—don't stop now." He let the simple statement speak for itself as his hand cupped her elbow and pushed her toward the bay horse. "Mount up."

Her cheeks were flame red as Joanna realized how brazen and immoral that sounded. With an angry little flounce, she spun away and stripped the reins from his hand. The muscles in her leg cramped when she attempted to lift her foot into the stirrup.

She had to grit her teeth against the soreness, but she was determined not to ask Linc for assistance. He was already astride the buckskin by the time she was able to pull herself into the bay's saddle.

She fired him an angry look and turned her horse, pointing it down the hill the same way they had come. "We're going this way," Linc stated. She glanced over her shoulder to see that he was heading in another direction. "It's a shortcut back to the road. We should be able to make it that far before we lose all the light." He explained why they were using a different route.

"Why didn't you say so?" she retorted and reined her horse in a semicircle to join up with him.

"You didn't ask," he said calmly and started his horse out at a brisk walk.

They traveled several yards before Joanna gave in to the need to defend her reputation. "For your information, I don't sleep around."

"I don't remember saying that you did," Linc replied with a brief glance.

"You seemed to have the impression that—"

He reined his horse to an abrupt halt and reached across to grab the reins of her mount, stopping it and leaning toward her. His level gaze seemed to bore into her.

"I don't see the point in conducting a post mortem. Nothing happened and nothing is likely to happen, so why don't we leave it at that."

She wanted to argue with him but he had removed any grounds for continuing the subject. His logic was irrefutable. She lowered her chin in a silent acknowledgment of the fact, signaling her agreement to his suggestion.

"Why do you have to make an issue out of everything, Joanna?" he sighed and released her horse's reins.

"I don't," she denied that as her horse started forward the instant the buckskin strided out.

"Yes, you do." There was a half-smile on his mouth and amusement in his glance. "In another two seconds, you're going to prove it by opening your mouth to argue that you don't argue over everything."

His statement forced her to keep silent, because it was precisely what she had been going to do. Only now she couldn't. His low chuckle indicated that he knew it.

"You think you're so smart, Linc Wilder," Joanna muttered in irritation. "But you're really not."

"I'm smart enough to know if we don't hurry it will be dark before we reach the road." He prodded his horse into a canter.

The bald knob of the mountain was still bathed in the golden light of the setting sun but the woods were casting longer and longer shadows. Joanna realized how quickly the twilight was encroaching when they rode into the trees. Allowing Linc to take the lead, she pulled her horse back and pointed its nose at the dappled hindquarters of the buckskin.

The deeper they went into the woods, the darker it became. What light there was in the forest seemed to be a pinkish gray. There was rustling of undergrowth and the rattling of tree limbs. An owl hooted, its eerie cry not sounding far away. Joanna admitted to being a little nervous.

They seemed to have traveled a long way. She was about to ask Linc how far it was to the road when she noticed the trees thinning out ahead of them. She breathed an unconscious sigh of relief when she saw the pale stretch of graveled road.

She checked her horse while Linc put the buckskin down the slight embankment to the road then let the bay gelding choose its own path. Once out of the trees, it didn't seem as dark as it had.

"Where are we?" she asked.

"Don't you recognize it?" He waved a hand down the road. "That's where you drove your car into the ditch to avoid Jessie."

"It doesn't look the same in this light," she said.

"The lane to his cabin is by that break in the trees." He pointed to it in his effort to orient her.

"I see it," she nodded.

Linc tipped his head back to look at the sky.

"It's a shame we don't have a moon tonight, but this half light should hold until we reach the cabin." He brought his chin down to look at her. "Now that we're on the road, it doesn't matter whether we have light. There will be enough for us to see. There isn't any reason to hurry unless you're anxious to get back."

"No. Not now that we're out of the woods," she replied.

By silent agreement, they kept their horses at a walk. The buckskin had a longer stride than Joanna's more closely coupled bay mount so it naturally stayed a little ahead of her all the time. She was less bothered by the nightsounds that came from the woods flanking the road.

The first stars were beginning to twinkle in the blue-gray sky. But the road continued to be a pale ribbon unwinding ahead of them. She became conscious of a cool draft against her skin and realized she hadn't tucked her blouse inside her jeans.

Letting the horse have its head, she wrapped the reins around the protruding horn of the saddle so her hands would be free. As she pushed her blouse inside the waistband, she became aware of the lengthening distance between her horse and the buckskin.

She was about to grab the reins when the bay jerked its head up and seemed to shudder beneath her. It snorted loudly and rolled a white eye toward the side of the woods just ahead of them. Her first glance only noticed the culvert but as her horse swung its head directly at it, she stared between the horse's ears. An eerie white cloud drifted gossamer-thin alongside the road by the culvert.

Terror gripped her throat. She blinked, certain her vivid imagination was playing tricks on her. But the funny bluish-white light remained and even wavered. She screamed and her horse bolted in panic, lunging straight at the buckskin.

"Linc!" Joanna called his name in panic.

Somehow he swung his horse to the side, avoiding a collision and reaching out for her at the same time. She grabbed for his neck and managed to kick her feet out of the stirrups as the bay horse ran out from under her. The buckskin danced nervously while she sobbed in frightened breaths and hung on tightly until his strong arms were able to sit her across the front of the saddle.

"It's a ghost! We've got to get out of here!" She buried her face in his shirt, digging her fingers into his shoulders.

"Joanna, what in heaven's name are you talking about?" His voice sounded caught between being amused and confused.

"Over there by the culvert," she whispered into the cloth of his shirt. "When my horse spooked, I looked between its ears and I saw it! Oh, let's get out of here!"

There was a moment of stillness, followed by the rumble of laughter deep in his chest. "Look. Is that what you saw, Joanna?" He tried very hard to keep the laughter inside.

His complete lack of concern forced her to peer toward the culvert. The light wavered and grew brighter. Her heart tumbled to her throat.

"Oh, my God, it's still there," she whispered, because she had expected it to be gone.

"That's foxfire."

Chapter Twelve

$\mathcal{H}$ is hand gripped the upper part of her arm and held her away from him, forcing Joanna to stop hiding her eyes. Shaken out of her wits by the experience, she was slow to register his words. Her eyes stayed closed and her teeth tightly clenched, her fingers curling into the hard flesh of his shoulders.

"Hey, did you hear me?" His chiding voice was low, rich with amusement. "It's only foxfire." Linc made it sound very harmless.

Braving the worst, she dragged her lashes open and rigidly focused her gaze on his face, still too frightened to look around. His hard features were gentled by contained humor and his eyes were warm with indulgent forbearance.

"Foxfire?" Her voice was a thin, wavering whisper.

"Marsh lights. It's a natural phenomenon—as opposed to the supernatural," he explained with a faint twinkle in his look.

By degrees, she inched her head around to slide an apprehensive peek at the mysterious glow. It seemed fainter, less ominous and frightening. It floated about waist high above the ditch, drifting toward the woods.

As she watched, the wispy phosphorescence grew smaller and gradually dissolved. A shudder went through her at its passing. She lowered her head and breathed in a shaky breath.

"I've never been so scared in all my life." The low admission germinated a seed of anger. It sprouted quickly and spread through her raw nerves. "Damn that Jessie Bates and his ghost-talk. Thanks to him, I've made a complete fool of myself again."

"You should be used to that," Linc suggested dryly.

His ready concurrence ran through her like a hot knife. Indignation swelled from the wound. "You really know how to make a person feel rotten, don't you?" Joanna charged.

He tipped back his head to let the laughter roll from his throat. It faded into a chuckle as he shifted her in his hold so that she was sitting crosswise in front of him. His head was tilted down, toward hers, a wide smile curving the line of his mouth. Her anger degenerated into a mild form of irritation and hurt pride.

"I don't think it's funny," she protested on a low, injured note.

"My momma always said a kiss makes the hurt go away," he murmured and bent his head, bringing his mouth against her lips. The pressure of his mouth was warm and mobile but all too brief. "Feel better?" Linc studied her with a laziness that said he knew well that she wanted more.

For that very reason, she wouldn't give him the satisfaction of admitting it. "Some." But her voice was shaky and she wondered if he could hear or feel the thudding of her pulse.

Her nerves were beginning to react to the hard contact with his muscled build. His left arm supported her back, the hand holding the reins pressed hard against the side of her hip. The palm and fingers of his right hand were curved to the outer portion of her thigh.

She could feel the strong rhythm of his heartbeat against her breast as she was molded sideways to his flatly muscled frame. It was a heady position with her hand resting on his shoulderbone to link fingers with the hand draped around his neck. There was a fleeting wish that she could stay this way for a little while longer.

Then she remembered, "My horse? It bolted." Instinctively her gaze swung to the road in search of her mount.

At a signal from its rider, the buckskin moved out at a walk, mincing a little at its double burden. "He's probably half-way to the barn by now," Linc answered. "We'll have to ride double. It isn't far to the cabin though."

The motion of the horse jabbed the saddlehorn into the tender flesh of her rump. Joanna winced and shifted her center of balance to avoid the prod of the horn. His strong hands assisted in the weight shift which brought her more fully against his body.

"Comfortable?" His downward glance was three-quarters lidded.

"Yes," Joanna assured him the problem had been solved.

In fact, she was quite comfortable. She silently reveled in this contact with his powerful build. She had never encountered any man who possessed this combination of keen intelligence and brute strength. She studied the rawly masculine features of his face. In her position, it would have required an effort not to look at him since she was squarely facing his profile.

When Linc noticed the way she contemplated him, Joanna felt the need to break the silence. "What causes foxfire?"

The situation was reversed and now she was the object of his steady regard. "It's a case of spontaneous combustion. Two elements can exist in the same environment with nothing happening until a spark sets them off—a catalyst of sorts." The run of his gaze over her face seemed to give another dimension to his explanation, something to do with their personal chemistries. "It's an elusive thing that is either there or it isn't," he finished.

173

It all became clear to her. The friction that was always between them, the physical attraction that kept pulling her to him, and the fire that was kindled within her when they came in contact, they all made sense.

As incredible as it seemed, she was falling in love with him, a man who could irritate her beyond belief yet could arouse a response that was more than mere passion. The dawning light of discovery shone in her eyes.

The air seemed to sizzle as his gaze locked with hers. His chest lifted with a breath that wasn't released. Then he was kissing her, roughly, possessively, crushing her hard to his body. An incredulous joy swept through her, heating her blood at this blatant demonstration of his desires after he had previously denied hers. It was strictly a reflex action that tightened the pressure on the bit to stop the horse.

The buckskin wasn't pleased with its double burden and impatient with its master who couldn't seem to make up his mind whether to stop or go. The animal tossed its head in agitation and pulled at the bit, snorting and shifting sideways in protest to the pressure.

As the horse began to act up, Linc was forced to break off the kiss and bring his fractious mount under control. His arm tightened protectively around Joanna until the horse settled down. He relaxed the pressure on the reins and the buckskin moved forward at a brisk walk.

"Do you suppose he was jealous?" Linc mocked.

"Maybe." Joanna contentedly nestled her head on his shoulder, enjoying the closeness.

"The next time I take you out we'll ride in a car," he stated.

A dreamy smile curved her mouth. "That sounds nice," she sighed.

They were nearly to the cabin when a flashlight beam swept the road in front of them. A second later, it was squarely in their eyes. Joanna turned her face into his shoulder to escape the blinding glare of light.

"Linc. Joanna. Are you all right?" Reece's voice came from the darkness behind the light. "Rachel and I heard a scream. A few minutes later a horse galloped by the cabin and through the pasture gate to your place. Was Joanna thrown? Is she hurt?"

"She's fine. She wasn't thrown," Linc assured him on that score. "She just had a little scare, that's all."

The focus of the beam was lowered to the road. "What a relief. We were coming out to find you and see if you needed any help," Reece explained as he approached the horse, accompanied by Rachel Parmelee. "What happened?"

"It's a long story. Joanna thought she saw a ghost," Linc explained with an underlying thread of amusement in his voice. "She screamed. Her horse spooked and nearly collided with mine. She sorta dived at me and I sorta grabbed." He swung out of the saddle and stepped to the ground, reaching up to lift Joanna down.

"You thought you saw a ghost?" There was the amusement of disbelief in her uncle's voice.

"Jessie Bates is to blame for that." Her hands were reluctant to leave Linc's shoulders. She had to force them down to her sides where she self-consciously smoothed them over her jeans.

"Jessie Bates?" Reece frowned in absolute confusion and looked from one to the other for an explanation.

"We stopped by his place while we were out riding." Linc collected the reins to lead his horse and walk along with the others. "Jessie told her a couple ghost stories and her imagination took over after that."

"It wasn't strictly my imagination," Joanna protested. "I did see something."

"What did you see?" Rachel's question prompted Joanna to notice that she and her uncle were holding hands.

It struck her as being a youthful display of affection, yet it also made her cognizant that she didn't possess the same easy confidence to display her affection for Linc so openly.

"There was some foxfire along the ditch, although I didn't know it was foxfire," she admitted her ignorance. "It was just an eerie light." She left out the part about looking between her horse's ears. It still made her feel silly when she thought about it. "After all the nonsense Jessie told us about ghosts, I thought that I was seeing one. That's when I screamed and the horse bolted and—" She let the explanation trail off and shrugged away her foolishness. She changed the subject. "How was the fishing?"

"We caught four nice bass for dinner," Reece answered.

"That 'we' happened to be 'me,'" Rachel corrected him in mock reproval.

"Didn't you catch any, Reece?" Joanna asked.

"I seemed to have trouble keeping my mind on fishing," he admitted and the look he gave Rachel identified the source of his distraction. "But we still made it a team effort. She caught them and I cooked them."

"And ate them all, I suppose?" Joanna teased.

"Yes," he admitted. "But we do have a fresh pot of coffee made. After your experience, you could probably do with a cup."

They had reached the driveway to the cabin and Linc stopped, the others automatically coming to a halt, too. "This is where I leave you," he announced casually.

"Aren't you coming in for coffee?" Joanna protested.

His head moved to the side in a single, negative shake. "There's a horse at the barn, waiting to be unsaddled."

She didn't want to say goodbye to him with Rachel and her uncle looking on, so she gently prompted them into leaving. "You go ahead. I'll be along directly."

After an exchange of good nights with Linc, her uncle and Rachel walked toward the lights of the cabin. Joanna watched them until they were out of hearing, then turned to Linc. He held her glance for an instant, then swung idly away to move to the left side of the buckskin and gather the reins in front of the pommel, preparing to mount. A sense of awkwardness had kept her silent but his action forced her to take the initiative.

"Will you be coming by tomorrow?" She tried to sound very light and casual.

"No, I'll be busy." Linc paused long enough to slide a glance over her, then stepped a foot into the stirrup and swung aboard. "You may be on vacation, but I've got a ranch to run," he reminded her.

"But—" She took a step toward him, her hand reaching out to touch his knee. The twilight was darkening, making it difficult to see his face.

"There are times when things happen so fast that you aren't sure what did happen—or why," Linc stated. "Think about it, Joanna, and be damned sure you know what you want."

"What if I said I was?" she protested.

"Then a couple of days won't change it," he reasoned. "You have a tendency to say things on the spur of the moment and regret them later. I don't want that to be the case this time." With a turn of his wrist, Linc reined his horse around Joanna. "Good night."

"Good night." She was a second slow in answering him, his comment about her impulsiveness hitting a little too close to home.

She watched until he had disappeared into the darkness, then turned to walk toward the cabin. She felt frustrated and denied, if only temporarily.

Chapter Thirteen

With the telephone receiver held tightly against her ear, Joanna chewed nervously at her lower lip and listened to the echo of the third ring on the other end of the line. Maybe it wasn't done in the Ozarks for a woman to call a man, but three days had gone by without a word from Linc. She simply couldn't wait any longer.

In the middle of the fourth ring, a woman's voice came on the line. "Hello?"

Startled by the female voice, Joanna hesitated, wondering if she had dialed the wrong number. "Is this . . . the Wilder ranch?"

"Yes, it is."

"May I speak to Linc Wilder, please?" she requested. Tension made her voice brisk to conceal her inner turmoil.

"I'm sorry, he isn't here right now," the woman's voice answered.

"Do you know where he is or when he'll be back?" Frustration scraped at her nerves as she tried not to let her disappointment show through her voice.

"He's got a sick calf. I think he went into the vet's to get some medicine for it. He didn't mention when he'd be back but I would imagine it will be sometime this morning yet," the woman answered a little vaguely.

"I see," Joanna murmured and absently glanced around the study, trying to decide what she should do.

"Did you want to leave your phone number? I can have him call you later," the woman suggested.

"Just . . . Just tell him Joanna called," she said finally.

"Joanna." The woman repeated her name. "I'll tell him."

"Thank you." She continued to hold the receiver after the line went dead, then hesitantly returned it to its cradle.

When footsteps approached the study, she heard them, but gave them little notice. It was her uncle's voice that finally penetrated her silent contemplation.

"There you are. Good morning." His greeting was bright and cheerful as he entered the room with a jaunty stride, a wide smile curving his mouth.

"Good morning." She breathed in deeply and

tried to shake free from the grayness of her spirit in the face of Reece's sunshine. Stirring from the chair behind the desk, she managed a smile. "I thought you would sleep in this morning."

"It's a beautiful day—much too beautiful to stay in bed," he insisted.

"Alone, you mean," Joanna teased, then shook her head. "How do you manage to look so rested when you haven't gotten home until after midnight three nights running?"

"Love is a wondrous tonic," he laughed.

The remark had been meant as a joke, but looking at him, Joanna was inclined to believe it was true. At least, it appeared to be true once the doubts were erased and that love was returned.

"At a glance, I'd say you discovered the fountain of youth," she smiled.

Reece laughed and his glance strayed to the telephone on the desk. "Were you on the phone just now?"

Her reaction was almost guilty. "Yes . . . I was," she admitted.

"You look upset. Was it your mother?" His expression became serious, etched with a fine trace of concern.

"No." She hesitated an instant. "Linc hasn't been around for a couple of days so I thought I'd call and invite him to dinner this evening. You don't mind, do you?"

"Of course not." His astute gaze read more into the response. "Is he coming?"

"He wasn't there. A woman answered and

said he'd gone to the veterinarian. A calf is sick, I guess," she admitted her failure to reach Linc.

Reece also read the silent question that was in her mind. "It probably was the lady who keeps house for him. He has someone come in twice a week to do the cleaning and laundry since his sister married." He casually passed on the information and watched her uncertainty fade.

"I left word that I called. He'll probably call later on," she said.

"I hope you didn't have anything planned for this morning," Reece stated. "I wanted you to go into town with me."

"There wasn't anything special I was going to do," she assured him. "I can come with you," although she hoped Linc didn't call while she was gone.

"Good." There was something very decisive about his voice and his smile. "Because I want you to help me choose a ring for Rachel."

"A ring," she repeated and eyed him uncertainly. "Do you mean a diamond ring—an engagement ring?"

"Yes."

Joanna smothered a laugh of surprise and delight. "Does Rachel know? Have you asked her?"

"Not yet," he admitted but without any sign of doubt about her answer. "First I want to buy the ring. You will come with me?"

"Wild horses couldn't stop me!" This was an event!

* * *

As they looked over the rings in the jeweler's case, they had a difference of opinion about the size and style of ring that would please Rachel. A week ago Joanna would have gone along with Reece's choice but Linc had influenced her thinking to a great extent.

"That one is beautiful," Reece conceded as Joanna held the diamond solitaire to the light, "but it is too plain, too simple. Look at the setting of this one." He drew her attention back to his choice. The center stone of the ring was approximately the same size as the single gem in the ring Joanna liked, but it was surrounded by a cluster of smaller diamonds. "It has such fire."

Aware of the jeweler patiently looking on, Joanna sighed. "Why don't you wait until the two of you can pick out the ring together?"

"No." Reece shook his head in a very definite rejection of that thought. "She would pick something simple and less expensive."

Joanna stared at him, a tiny smile creeping around the corners of her mouth. "Do you realize what you just said?" she murmured. Amusement danced in her eyes when he met her look.

"But I want to buy her something—" He stopped to consider the problem.

Joanna put the problem into words. "You have to decide whether you are going to buy a ring that *you* want or one that *she* wants."

He hesitated, sighed, and cast a resigned glance at the jeweler. "I will take the solitaire."

"She'll love it." Joanna smiled her approval as the jeweler moved away from the glass case to write up the sales ticket. "And she is the one who has to wear it."

When the transaction was completed and they were walking out of the jewelry store, Joanna asked, "When are you going to propose to her? Tonight?"

"Yes." It was a somewhat clipped answer.

She studied him with a sidelong glance, surprised to see the lines of tension around his mouth and eyes. It was the first time she had ever seen Reece appear nervous. It was touching in a man usually so confident of himself.

"Where to, now?" She changed the subject in an effort to relax him. "What about some lunch? It's a little early but we'll miss the noon crowd."

He came to an abrupt stop on the sidewalk, his hesitancy vanishing as he came to a decision. "No. I can't wait until tonight. I'm going to ask her now."

"But . . . isn't she working?" Joanna was thrown by his sudden change of plans.

"Yes." With a quick, purposeful stride, he started for the car parked at the curb. "We'll drive to her shop."

"Wouldn't it be better to wait until she takes her lunch break?" Joanna suggested and had to hurry to keep up with him. He was already sliding behind the wheel before she had the passenger door open. "She'll probably be busy with customers and all," Joanna reasoned.

"The store is always competing with me for her time. I am not going to allow it to dictate when it would be convenient for a proposal of marriage."

The engine was started and Reece was shifting in reverse when she closed her car door. The determined set of his jaw left her in no doubt that his mind had been made up.

"Aren't you rushing things just a little, Reece?" she wondered.

"When I leave the Ozarks at the end of the month, Rachel is going to come with me as my wife," he stated. "That doesn't allow much time to find a competent manager to take over the store. I have no intention of leaving without her and I know Rachel won't go unless she is assured it is running smoothly. And she won't begin to look for someone until I have proposed."

"Wouldn't it be simpler if she sold it?" It seemed the logical solution to Joanna. In the long run, there would be fewer headaches.

"It would be simpler, yes," Reece agreed. "But it represents security and independence to Rachel. I don't expect her to give it up for me."

When he explained it, Joanna could see that he was right. Eventually Rachel would feel lost if she didn't remain involved with the store's operation, even if it had to be at a distance. It had occupied too much of her life for it to be suddenly cut out of it without leaving a void that not even Reece's love could fill.

Slowing the car, he turned into the parking lot by the shop. He parked it in an empty space and switched off the engine. "Are you coming in?" He paused with the door open to glance at Joanna.

She smiled faintly. "No, I think you'll have plenty of witnesses without me along." It broke the tension in his expression and he returned the smile. "Good luck," she called to him as he climbed out of the car.

There were more than a dozen customers in the store when Reece entered. Nervously he turned the ring box around in his hand and glanced around the store. He saw her standing behind the counter near the cash register and experienced that rush of sweet pleasure lift him. For the run of several seconds, he was content just to look at her.

As if feeling his eyes on her, Rachel looked up and noticed him on the opposite side of the room. He watched her expression change, the special warmth that entered her gaze and the smile that was reserved just for him. He crossed to the counter.

"Hello. How are you today?" Her look and tone of voice made the trite phrase sound much more meaningful and intimate.

"Fine." He was conscious of the people around them and wished, not for the first time, that he could order them out and have this woman all to himself.

"Was there something you wanted?" Again the inquiry appeared very innocent, a clerk to a customer.

Reece smiled widely. "Yes, there is but for the time being, I'll be satisfied with five minutes of your time."

She laughed a little self-consciously, and he enjoyed the warm sound of it. There was a freshness to her that had nothing to do with age. Her gaze made an appraising sweep of the shop and its customers. A dark-haired woman was studying a group of Kewpie dolls in a display case.

"Excuse me just a minute," Rachel apologized to Reece and moved down the counter. "Was there something you'd like to see?"

"Yes, please. The second doll from the left." The woman pointed to the one she meant. "I have three nieces who collect dolls," the woman explained as Rachel opened the case and brought out the doll to show her. "I want to bring them back something to add to their collection."

"This one is very popular," Rachel assured the brunette, but her gaze strayed to Reece standing by the cash register, showing where her attention was truly focused at the moment.

"I'll definitely take that one," the woman decided. "Why don't you just give me three?" She held up three fingers.

"Certainly. Is there anything else?"

"I'd like to look around a little more," the woman smiled.

"Go right ahead," Rachel encouraged her to browse. "The dolls will be at the cash register."

While she was taking the three dolls from the stock below the counter, Reece inobtrusively opened the ring box and set it on the glass shelf near the cash register. She didn't glance in that direction when she walked back to box the three dolls. "I can't promise you five minutes all at one time. Will you settle for a minute here and there?" she asked with a smile.

"I bought something for you." Reece went straight to the point, gesturing toward the ring with a nod of his head. Her eyes widened when she saw it. They became misty as they swung to him, her lips parted in wordless surprise. "Don't ring up a 'No Sale.'"

Her laugh was slightly choked by emotion. "Is this a proposal?" Her hand pushed at the side of her hair, but she made no move to reach for the ring.

"It very definitely is." He could stand it no longer and removed the ring from the velvet case. Her hand was shaking as she extended it toward him. "Does that mean you are accepting?"

"Yes," she said in a breathless voice. He slipped it on her finger, then held her hand tightly, his gaze burrowing into her. "Oh, Reece, you do pick the darnedest places. First the boat, with me looking a sight, and now here."

The ache in her voice told him that she wanted

to be in his arms, that she wanted to be kissed by him. She wasn't alone in her frustration.

"I was going to wait until tonight and do it properly with candlelight and wine and beautiful music in the background," Reece admitted. "I had a very romantic setting all planned. But I wanted you to say 'yes' because I asked you and not because you were caught up in the mood of the moment."

Her response to that was a vague shake of her head, then she was leaning across the counter, her hand curving behind the back of his neck. She kissed him without reserve, erasing any doubt about the reason behind her acceptance.

There was absolute silence in the shop when their kiss ended. All attention was obliquely focused on them. Reece turned, beaming proudly as he surveyed the customers. "It is all perfectly respectable," he informed them. "The lady has just consented to marry me."

A murmur ran through the store, rippling like a happy wave. There were smiles of understanding and silent wishes of happiness in their eyes.

Chapter Fourteen

Outside the doll shop, the suspense was building. Waiting in the car with the windows rolled down, Joanna watched the store entrance. Time passed slowly, its weight heavy on her hands. Her thoughts wandered in and around the subject of love and marriage. She tried to imagine her mother's reaction to someone like Linc without success, but it was easy to visualize her skepticism at the thought of Reece finally settling down. She wouldn't take the news well.

With the constant flow of summer traffic on the busy street, the crunching sound of tires on the graveled parking lot attracted minimal attention from Joanna. There was vague recognition that a vehicle had driven up to park next to the car. Her glance strayed to the side when a door was opened. An electric shock tingled through her system at the sight of Linc's rangy build filling her vision.

"Hello." Resting a hand on top of the car, he bent to look in the opened window and treated her to one of his crooked smiles.

Her heart seemed to tumble over her ribs with reckless abandon. "Hello." There was a slightly breathless quality to her voice.

"I was driving by and recognized the car. I thought I noticed someone sitting in it." He looked briefly toward the shop. "I take it Reece is inside."

"Yes." It seemed much longer than three days since she had seen him. An inexplicable kind of hunger filled her and she feasted her eyes on his virile features carved in bronze.

His glance returned to her, his golden-brown eyes inspecting her in a way that threw her senses into chaos. "Have you managed to stay out of trouble lately? No more run-ins with any mules or ghosts?" He was mocking her, yet with a warmth and subtle humor that made it something special.

"Things like that only seem to happen to me when you're around," Joanna replied. "My life is relatively sane otherwise."

"Implying that I make you a little crazy?" Linc rephrased the statement.

It did seem to explain the wild, wonderful feeling raging inside her—crazy in love. "Yes."

She agreed with him without elaborating on the source of this glorious madness.

"Is that good or bad?" His searching gaze probed her expression in an attempt to uncover the ulterior meaning he seemed to sense existed.

"I think it could be good," Joanna admitted but it depended so much on how he felt.

A lazy gleam of satisfaction appeared in his gaze before his attention was distracted. "Here comes Reece with Rachel," he announced as he straightened to stand erect.

One look at the beaming couple told Joanna what Rachel's answer had been. Each had an arm around the other's waist as they approached the parked car. As Joanna opened the door and stepped out, Linc moved to one side to give her room.

"She said 'yes,' didn't she?" Joanna directed the unnecessary question to her uncle, already positive of the answer.

"She did," Reece stated proudly, then informed Linc of their engagement. "Rachel has agreed to marry me."

"Welcome to the family." Joanna hugged her aunt-to-be, while Linc shook hands with Reece.

"Congratulations."

For the next couple of minutes, it was a jumble of voices as they talked over each other until none of it made sense. They all seemed to realize it simultaneously and stopped talking. The abrupt silence brought a round of shared laughter.

"This calls for a party to celebrate the occasion," Linc stated when it stopped.

"Linc is right," Joanna agreed. "Dinner, champagne, everything."

"Actually, I had in mind an old-fashioned barbeque at my place," he corrected her with an amused glance. "I'll invite a bunch of friends and neighbors over Sunday afternoon."

"There's no need to go to such trouble," Reece protested.

"If I thought it would be too much trouble, I wouldn't have suggested it," Linc replied. "I'll arrange it for Sunday . . . unless the two of you plan to keep the engagement a secret for a while."

"It would be extremely difficult." A smile dimpled Rachel's mouth. "Everyone in the store knows about it. By this afternoon, it will be all over town."

"I wouldn't have cared if the whole world had been there," Reece insisted.

Linc slid a glance at his watch. "I need to be leaving," he said indicating there was somewhere else he had to be. His glance rested on Joanna. "Would you give me a hand planning the menu for Sunday?"

"Sure," she agreed without hesitation.

"I'll stop by this evening sometime," he told her and turned his attention to the engaged couple. "Congratulations again."

"Come for dinner," Joanna invited, betraying some of her eagerness for his company.

Linc shook his head as he opened the door to

the pickup cab. "I can't make it tonight but I'll see you later in the evening."

His departure signaled the close of the gathering. Rachel reluctantly heeded the silent summons of the shop, calling her back to work. All three of them were looking forward to the coming night, but not all for the same reasons.

When Linc arrived that night, Reece had already left the cabin to meet Rachel. Their initial conversation centered on the engagement of her uncle who was his best friend and their shared approval of it. It naturally led into his plans for the Sunday barbeque and a discussion of the menu. As he made notes, Joanna was beginning to think it was the sole reason he was there, that it hadn't been an excuse to see her as she had first hoped.

She hardly paid attention when Linc read the list back to her. "If that isn't enough variety to satisfy everyone's likes and dislikes, they can just go hungry," he concluded on a mock threat. "Wouldn't you say so?"

"What?" The blankness left her expression as she remembered what he'd said. "Yes, that's right."

His gaze traveled over her, then he set his notes aside and combed his fingers through his hair. Flexing his shoulder muscles, he rolled leisurely to his feet and took a step away from the couch. Curled in an armchair, Joanna looked up in bewildered protest.

"Are you leaving?" she questioned.

"Why? Do you want me to go?" With an eyebrow raised he halted near her chair. The subdued glitter in his look said he already knew the answer.

She was irritated into pretending an indifference that she didn't feel. "No, but naturally, if you have somewhere else to go, I don't expect you to stay just to keep me company." She shrugged and challenged him. "Do you?"

"No." A smile showed briefly.

She never knew how to act with him. He kept changing the pace and course of their relationship until she didn't know what to expect next. Since she wasn't able to second-guess him, she stopped trying.

"There's iced tea in the kitchen. Would you like some?" She'd get a crick in her neck if she had to keep looking up at him so Joanna uncrossed her legs and rose from the chair.

"I'm glad you did that," Linc said.

His remark made no sense at all. "Did what?" she frowned, because to her knowledge, she had done nothing except offer him a cold drink.

"Stood up." The span of a foot separated them.

"Why?" Joanna still didn't understand. If anything, she was more confused.

"There is an old Ozark superstition," his hands found her waist and shortened some of that distance, "—that says a man shouldn't kiss a girl while he's standing and she's sitting in a chair."

The nearness of him was starting those funny

little pitter-patters of her heart. With an absent fascination, she studied the way her hands rested on the wall of his chest.

"Why not?" The upward sweep of her glance met his steady look and all sorts of crazy sensations started leaping inside.

"According to superstition, that would cause an immediate quarrel," Linc explained.

"Who told you that?" She laughed out the words.

"I have it on the best authority," he assured her.

"Let me guess. Jessie Bates." She tipped her head to one side, provocative and challenging.

"Right, and arguing is not one of the things I want to do with you tonight," Linc stated and increased the pressure to bring her fully against him.

It was all the invitation Joanna needed as she stretched to meet him halfway. His mouth seared its claim on hers in a long, drugging kiss. Arching against him, she was aware of his hard, muscular thighs and the sinewed steel of his encircling arms molding her to him. Her hands curled themselves around his neck, her anchor in this raging storm of emotions.

When they finally came up for air, Joanna was too dazzled by the heat lightning flashing through her to move an inch away from him. The brush of his lips closed her eyes, flirting with her lashes before it ran over the rest of her face. The emotion running through her was so fierce that she trembled from it.

She wanted him so much that when she spoke, it was almost a groan. "Linc, you can't believe any more that I'm not ready." It was a protest at his lack of initiative to let the embrace go beyond mere kisses.

"By God, you'd better mean that," he muttered against her throat. "I'm not interested in casual sex, Joanna. If that's all you want, you're picking the wrong man."

"I think I have the right one," she said and felt a brief stirring of surprise that she could be so positive. "I barely know you at all, yet I seem to know all that's important."

His hand covered her breast in a physical demonstration of the rights she was giving him. "Patience is not one of my strong suits," Linc warned. "If you think I'm going to be like Reece and court you for nearly six years, you're wrong. It isn't going to be like that."

"I don't want it like that," Joanna admitted huskily. "I couldn't stand it."

She felt she would go crazy now if he didn't do more than hold her. Her breast seemed to swell to fill the palm of his hand, straining to achieve a greater intimacy. All of her ached with the same need.

"I'm not going to carry on any love affair long distance—with you in California and me here." He continued to spell out his conditions, insisting that Joanna be aware of what he expected.

"What is the alternative to long distance?" She was arching against him in deliberate provocation. Her teeth teased at his earlobe, nipping at it in sexual play. "Is it this? You're from Missouri, Linc. Show me."

"It won't be a temporary coupling." Linc drew his head back to look at her while he emphasized his message. "The linkage will be a lasting one."

Her lips lay against each other in an inviting line, sensual and full. "Ever since I arrived in the Ozarks, everyone has been telling me how instinctively intelligent you hillpeople are. But I'm beginning to think I'll have to send you an engraved invitation to make love to me." She didn't try to hide any of her feelings from him, letting him see all the fires that burned inside. "I thought you were a man of action. But, maybe you act as slow as you talk."

"Are you trying to get a rise out of me?" Linc drawled and eyed her with a complacent look.

"Now, you're getting the idea, " she murmured.

His mouth began its movement toward her. "I'll give you all you can handle—and more," he taunted.

The piercing crush of his arms was sweet agony, that unique mixture of pleasure and pain. There was no holding back in this embrace. Joanna wanted to give as she got, and Linc was inflaming her with his needs.

The shrill ring of the telephone was a piercing interruption. Joanna shuddered a protest when Linc lifted his head, dragging his mouth across her temple. Leaning against him, she tried to close her hearing to the sound, but it kept repeating itself.

His arm stayed around her waist, supporting her and drawing her along with him as he turned to pick up the receiver. With her head tipped to rest against his shoulder, Joanna watched him carry the phone to his ear and answer it.

"No, it isn't. Reece isn't here at the moment," Linc said in an obvious response to a question by the caller.

During the subsequent pause, Joanna was conscious of the firm possession of the arm curved around her. She liked the feel of it, the implication of belonging to him.

"Yes, Joanna is here." Linc passed the receiver to her.

She took it with every intention of quickly getting rid of the caller. "Hello." Her tone was aloof, designed to discourage conversation.

"Joanna, what is going on there? Who was that man who answered the phone?" her mother's voice demanded.

She went rigid with surprise, stiffening self-consciously in Linc's possessive hold. "Mother! I wasn't expecting you to call." It had been the farthest thing from her mind when the phone had rung.

"I had that impression when the man answered the phone." There was a quality of disdain in her voice. "You haven't told me who he is yet?"

"That was Linc. Linc Wilder." Joanna quickly added his full name and shifted out of the loose hold of his arm. Even though her mother couldn't see the casually intimate embrace, she had been influenced by other times when her mother had come along on similar scenes.

"I'm sure Reece probably has mentioned him to you," Joanna continued and felt a sudden chill in the air. Her side glance caught the coolness of Linc's expression as he quietly studied her.

Turning aside, he wandered to the fireplace and lit a cigarette. Her glance followed him, then fell when he looked back. He was making her feel small for not claiming any personal relationship with him. It wasn't a comfortable sensation.

"I swear I will never understand why Reece vacations in such a godforsaken spot, so removed from all the conveniences," her mother decried her brother-in-law's choice. "That drawling hillbilly can't provide the kind of stimulating company Reece can find here in L.A.—or anywhere else for that matter."

Joanna bristled in defense of the Ozarks, the cabin, and Linc. "You can't know that. You've never met him, Mother. And Linc is here so we could plan the menu for Sunday's barbeque we're having for Reece and Rachel."

"Who is Rachel?" The question was quick and immediate.

"Haven't you heard?" Joanna asked with false innocence, fully aware there hadn't been time for her mother to be informed about the engagement.

"Heard what?" There was impatience in the voice on the line.

"I think I should let Reece tell you himself," Joanna replied.

"Tell me what? Joanna, will you please stop being so mysterious and tell me what is going on out there?" her mother demanded.

"Reece is engaged." She knew she was dropping a bombshell so she wasn't surprised by the explosion.

"Engaged? That's absurd! To whom?" There was a mixture of doubt and challenge.

"To Rachel Parmelee."

"Who is Rachel Parmelee?" It sounded like a request for her pedigree.

"She owns a retail store here in the area," Joanna explained. "I think you'll like her, Mother. She is a lovely, intelligent woman—a widow." The last was added in all seriousness.

"She is from the Ozarks?"

"Yes."

"Why on earth is Reece marrying her?" Her mother still didn't quite believe it. "He's been a bachelor all these years. Why should he get married now?"

"Mother, when you see them together, you won't have to ask that question," Joanna assured her.

"I have known Reece considerably longer than you have, Joanna," her mother retorted dryly. "There have been countless affairs over the years. The instant the newness wears off, Reece casts them aside. He has never been so foolish as to become engaged before." She altered her tactic to inquire, "When is this supposed marriage to take place?"

"I don't remember a date being mentioned." Which was true, but something kept her from relating to her mother how soon Reece intended to marry Rachel. "You'll have to ask Reece."

"I will." It was a very definite reply. "Where is he?"

"With Rachel. I'm not sure what time he'll be back," Joanna admitted. "Why did you call, Mother? You never have said."

"I haven't heard from you. You haven't written or called. Naturally I wanted to find out what was going on there. There seems to be a great deal more than I expected," she replied, more than a little miffed that she hadn't been kept more closely informed.

Joanna slid a glance at Linc and watched him take a drag on the cigarette, then toss the butt in the charred-black hearth of the fireplace. As he turned his head to look at her, she dropped her gaze.

"I don't mean to seem rude, Mother, but I can't talk any longer. I do have company," she reminded her. "I'm sure Reece will be calling you in the next day or two anyway."

"Your message is very clear. I won't keep you from entertaining your guest." There was an acid trace of sarcasm in her reply. "Goodbye, Joanna."

"Goodbye." Her hand was wrapped tightly around the receiver, her knuckles showing white as she hung up the phone.

Why did she let her mother do this to her? She glanced toward the fireplace and encountered Linc's steady gaze. Hooking her thumbs in the loops of her jeans, Joanna wandered in that direction.

"That was my mother on the phone," she explained.

"So I gathered," he murmured dryly. "I had the impression she wasn't pleased to hear about the engagement."

"Yes, well, it came as quite a surprise to her," she admitted, a little defensive about her mother's reaction. "Naturally she was a little stunned."

"What's your mother like?" Linc studied her with a vaguely absent look.

That wasn't an easy question to answer. "She's . . . sophisticated, beautiful . . . very self-confident . . . and"—Joanna paused, one corner of her mouth lifting at a wry angle—"and determined to have her own way in nearly everything." She looked at him. "Why?"

But Linc didn't directly respond to her question, remarking instead, "I imagine she celebrates special occasions with champagne dinners."

"She does," Joanna admitted and defended it. "Barbeques are fun, but you have to admit they aren't exactly romantic."

An eyebrow lifted in silent skepticism. "I

guess that depends on whether you are the barbeque or champagne type." He picked up his hat.

Joanna gave him a startled look. "Are you leaving now?"

"Yes."

"But—" How could he?

"You need to give some thought to which type you are—barbeque or champagne." Linc stated quietly and adjusted the hat low on his forehead. "Good night, Joanna."

Chapter Fifteen

$\mathcal{H}$ er sandaled feet lightly skimmed over the steps as Joanna hurried downstairs. There was no sign of Reece in the living room. She scanned the doorways for a clue to his whereabouts.

"Reece! Are you ready to pick up Rachel?" she called and started across the living room to expand her search for him. "Not yet," he answered, but Joanna couldn't place the direction of his voice. "I'm on the porch, having a cup of coffee. Come join me."

With that information, she altered her course to walk to the screen door facing the lake. As she pushed it open, she saw him seated in one of the wicker chairs. A water-cooled breeze drifted in from the lake, but the late morning was turning warm and somnolent.

She let the screen door shut and advanced toward her uncle. The white slacks and knit shirt of navy blue enhanced his dark good looks and his trimly masculine build.

"When are you leaving to pick up Rachel?" she asked.

"I didn't plan to leave for another twenty minutes. Why?" His glance was mildly curious.

"I told Linc we'd be there a little early," she explained.

"Certainly." He nodded and would have added more but a noise intruded on nature's stillness. They exchanged questioning looks.

"It sounds like a car just drove in. I'll go see who it is," Joanna said and turned to the screen door.

There was a vaguely puzzled frown in her expression as she entered the cabin. Since the road came to a dead end a quarter mile further, they didn't get passing traffic or the idle sightseer stopping to ask for directions.

As she crossed the room, she heard the idling of a car motor out front and the slam of a door. The front door was open to allow cross-ventilation but the dark mesh of its screen door didn't give Joanna a clear view outside until she was all the way to the door.

Her eyes widened in surprised shock at the sight of the slimly elegant woman approaching the cabin. Dressed in an expensive beige suit and a brightly striped silk blouse, she was the epitome of breezy sophistication. Her artfully bleached blonde hair was a shade lighter than

Joanna's sun-streaked hair and styled in a loose coil. She was tanned to a golden color that took years off her age.

"Mother!" Joanna finally found her voice and the strength to open the screen door. "How did you get here?" It was a ridiculous question since the taxi was just now reversing out of the drive.

"After that ride, a pack train couldn't have been more uncomfortable." There was a stinging acidity to her dry answer.

"What are you doing here?" Joanna was still trying to recover from the astonishment of her mother's unexpected appearance. "Why didn't you let us know you were coming?"

"Isn't it obvious that I came to see you and find out for myself just what's going on here?" her mother challenged and handed Joanna the camel-brown weekender bag she was carrying. As she entered the cabin, her disdainful glance made a sweep of the surroundings. "I must admit I'm finding it difficult to see what it is you find to like about this place. After two weeks, I would be bored to tears. There's nothing but hills and trees; the roads were wretched—"

Her bronze-tinted lips were parted to add more disparaging remarks, but she stopped, distracted by something she saw. As her expression slowly changed to an aloof and challenging smile, Joanna looked around to see the "something" was Reece.

"Hello, Reece." There was a silken smoothness to her mother's greeting. "Surprised to see me?"

A brittle tension crackled through the room as the pair faced each other, familiar antagonists meeting again. There was a silent weighing of each other before Reece smoothly crossed the room to greet her.

"I wasn't expecting you but I truly can't say that I'm surprised to see you." He kissed the smooth cheek she offered him.

"Joanna tells me that congratulations are in order." She arched him a look of amusement. "I always thought you were too clever to be caught. Who would have thought a hillbilly would succeed in snaring you when so many have tried? I'm definitely looking forward to meeting your 'Daisy Mae' while I'm here."

Joanna stiffened at her mother's thinly disguised insults of Reece's choice for a wife, masked only by a taunting smile and the amusement in her softly cultured voice. Except for the hardening line of his smile, Reece gave no other outward indication that her mother's barbed references to Rachel had inflicted any damage.

"I have the feeling Rachel will find it as much of a pleasure as you do." He easily parried her remarks with a jibe of his own. Joanna saw the flash of irritation in her mother's eyes that he hadn't risen to the bait, but the fire was quickly banked. "As a matter of fact, I have to leave shortly to pick up Rachel. A friend of ours is having a party for us this afternoon to celebrate our engagement."

"I believe Joanna made some reference to that when I talked to her on the phone the other evening." Her mother pretended to vaguely recall the reference to the barbeque. "I suppose it will be one of those homespun affairs with all the grannies and the kissin' cousins there. Do you suppose they'll mind if I attend? I wouldn't want to miss it."

"Linc would not object at all," Reece assured her without blinking an eye.

"I suppose that was a silly question. After all, country people are known for their hospitality." Instead of making that a trait to be admired, she managed to imply it was quaintly stupid.

Joanna was finding it difficult to keep her temper in the face of all these snide references to the questionable worth of the Ozark natives. Aware that her attitude had been initially the same, regarding them as country bumpkins, she held her silence.

"When did you arrive, Mother?" Joanna couldn't recall that there had been an early flight scheduled from California.

"Late last night. I'm certainly glad I spent the night in a hotel instead of coming directly here. The taxi would never have been able to find this place in the dark. He charged me extra just for traveling over these roads in the daylight." She again implied her disdain for the location.

"You should have phoned from the airport. We would have picked you up," Joanna replied, "and saved you from paying a taxi to come all this way."

"And spoil my surprise?" she countered. "That would have taken the fun out of it." She brought her attention back to Reece. "I have to confess I was curious why you have kept coming here year after year. Now that I've seen it, I'm still baffled over what attracts you to this place."

"Perhaps because there is nothing artificial here," Reece suggested. "Not the scenery or the people."

Joanna flashed a quick glance at her mother to see her reaction to his insinuation that she was phony. There was the faintest crack in her mother's smiling expression, a whisper of indication in the softly indrawn breath.

Then Reece was inclining his head in mock deference to her mother and excusing himself. "I must let Rachel know I have been delayed a few minutes."

"She has you jumping through hoops already, doesn't she?" her mother mocked at his retreating back as Reece walked toward the study. With Reece gone from the room, she stopped trying to hide her intense displeasure behind the mask of a false smile. "He may have gotten himself engaged to this country yokel, but he'll never marry her."

"Mother, you aren't being fair. You haven't even met Rachel," Joanna protested impatiently with her mother's superior attitude.

"Rachel. Even her name sounds common," her mother declared in contempt. Aware the remark had spurred Joanna's temper, her mother pressed a hand to her forehead as if in pain. "Please, Joanna, I'm not in the mood to argue. After bouncing all over that road, my head is pounding. Does this rustic little hideaway possess a bathroom where I could freshen up after that dusty drive? God, how I dread traveling over that again. My nerves are shot."

Smothering her anger, Joanna turned toward the stairs. "I'll show you to my room in the loft. It has a private bath." She passed on the information in a curt voice. "We'll be leaving soon for the party. Would you rather stay here and rest? We can always send someone to get you later on."

"I wouldn't dream of causing Reece any inconvenience," she stated. "I'll ride along with him to save him the extra trip. Besides, I'd rather meet this Rachel when there aren't a lot of other people around."

Joanna didn't find that to be a very heartening statement but Reece took it in stride when he learned about it as if he had guessed it all along. Every remark seemed to have a sharp side.

When Reece stopped the car in front of a small bungalow on a tree-shaded residential street, Rachel must have been watching for him because she was out the front door before Reece stepped out of the car.

"Is this where she lives?" Elizabeth eyed the small dwelling with a trace of contempt.

Reece paused long enough to reply. "Yes, until we are married. Then she will live where I do."

Joanna observed the rigidness of her mother's features as she watched the couple meet on the sidewalk, the radiance that seemed to envelop both of them. Rachel's unerring clothes sense had chosen a sundress that was summery and mature in design. It was navy blue with white polkadots, a dark shade that complimented her creamy complexion.

"Rachel isn't what you expected is she, Mother? Joanna murmured. "I mean, she isn't exactly a hick."

"She isn't exactly worldly or sophisticated either, which is the type of wife Reece needs," her mother retorted in an equally low voice.

Once both were in the car, Reece made the introductions. Rachel seemed oblivious to the veiled hostility that laced the tone of Joanna's mother.

As Reece drove away from the curb, Elizabeth leaned forward. "After meeting you, Rachel, I wonder if you realize how extremely lucky you are?"

"I think I do." Rachel cast a warm glance at Reece and smiled.

Joanna watched her mother stiffen with jealousy, then control. "I do hope you let me help with the wedding plans," she addressed both of them, managing to sound very pleasant. "Have you two set the date?"

"Next week," Reece answered.

Elizabeth blanched at the answer, and Joanna felt sorry for her. It couldn't be easy for her. Yet, she recovered with remarkable aplomb.

"It's going to be very simple," Rachel elaborated on their plans. "Just the minister and two witnesses."

"Reece," her mother directed her protest at

him. "That isn't fair to cheat all your friends and family out of a wedding after we've waited so long." She directed a false smile at Rachel. "Not to mention your bride. I'm sure Rachel would like something a little more elaborate."

"Not me," Rachel declared with a faint laugh. "It's too much wear and tear on the nerves."

"Oh, speaking of wear and tear on the nerves—" Elizabeth switched the subject, talking to Reece and ignoring Rachel altogether. "I saw Grace Whittington the other day, Reece. She and Alex are having their annual summer party next month. You know, the usual black tie affair."

Joanna was astounded. She had never known her mother to be so flagrantly rude before. She was trying to put Rachel in the position of being the outsider, talking about people and events she was unfamiliar with, and a kind of life she'd never known.

"Naturally the Governor will be there. Sylvia was telling me that—" Elizabeth continued to rattle on, dropping names and titles, sounding disgustingly snobbish.

Joanna glanced at her uncle behind the wheel, wondering why he didn't say something. His handsome features were grim, but Reece remained silent. Joanna marveled at the control he exercised over his temper. She guessed that Rachel was the reason he said nothing. They were on their way to their engagement party. Reece didn't want any harsh words to mar the event.

Her mother's monopoly of the conversation made it a long drive to the Wilder ranch. Joanna was relieved when it came into view.

There were already more than a dozen vehicles parked in the ranch yard when they arrived, and more guests driving in behind them. Music and happy voices were coming from the rear patio area of the sprawling house. Circling around the building, they joined the party in progress.

A tent canopy was set up on the lawn to offer shade from the sun, but most of the guests had gathered on the redwood sundeck of the patio where the beer and cold drinks were located. The patio gave a hundred and eighty degree view of the lake below and the blue line of hills.

"This is quite a place," her mother murmured in an aside to Joanna.

Irritated by her previously condescending attitude toward the Ozarks and its inhabitants, Joanna couldn't resist scoring one for the other side. "It's just a typical hillbilly shack, Mother." She saw Linc engaged in a conversation with one of the guests and quickened her pace, moving ahead of her mother to greet him. "Hello! How come you started the party without the guests of honor?"

She had to force the light banter into her greeting, because she wasn't anxious for the moment when she would have to introduce Linc to her mother. But it couldn't be avoided.

"I was beginning to think you weren't going to

make it." Linc separated himself from the other guests and crossed the lawn to meet the four of them.

Although the comment was addressed to all of them, his gaze singled Joanna out. His arm curved itself quite naturally around her waist as he shook hands to welcome Reece and Rachel and turned expectantly toward the fourth member of the group.

Aware that her mother had taken due note of the familiar possession by Linc, Joanna began the introductions. "This is our host, Linc Wilder." Tension made her smile stiff. "I'd like you to meet my mother, Elizabeth Morgan. She arrived unexpectedly this morning to surprise us."

Although nothing changed in Linc's expression, she sensed an added alertness about him. "Welcome to the Ozarks, Mrs. Morgan. I believe we talked briefly the other evening."

"Yes, you answered the phone the night I talked to Joanna." Her mother made a show of recalling the incident as if it had been hardly worthy of her notice.

"I have been waiting to meet you," Linc said, "but I didn't think the opportunity would come so soon."

"Oh, really?" She was none too pleased by the comment and Joanna mentally braced herself for the scathing remarks that would come.

But Linc didn't give her a chance to reply further, nor satisfy her curiosity as to his reason. "Perhaps we'll have a chance to talk later. Right now, I think we should join the others. I know they're anxious to offer their congratulations to Reece and Rachel."

He kept Joanna firmly at his side while they walked to the patio. Reece and Rachel were quickly engulfed in a tide of well-wishers. Standing next to Linc with her mother to one side, Joanna couldn't shake the feeling of alarm over his proposed conversation with her mother.

"This is quite a gathering, Mr. Wilder," her mother remarked.

"Linc," he corrected. "We aren't formal in the Ozarks."

Her glance made a disparaging sweep of the casually dressed crowd. "So I've noticed," she murmured dryly.

But Linc didn't take any notice of the veiled contempt in her mother's reply. He glanced instead at Joanna. "There's some people I'd like you to meet." Her mother was included in the statement. The hand on her waist guided her in the direction of two couples standing nearby. "This is my sister, Sharon, and her husband, Dick Scott."

He introduced them first to the young, dark-haired couple. Joanna was a little surprised that his sister was such a petite thing. The resemblance to her brother was very slight. The second couple was older, closer to Linc's age.

"—and Tanya and Jake Lassiter," Linc continued the introduction, concluding with, "Meet Mrs. Morgan and her daughter, Joanna."

There was a murmur of exchanged greetings, then his sister, Sharon, focused a sparkling look on Joanna. "Linc has mentioned you a couple of times. I'm glad I've finally gotten to meet you."

"Thank you—I think," Joanna qualified her answer, unsure what Linc might have said about her.

"Oh, it was all good," Sharon assured her and cast a sly glance at her older brother. "Very interesting, in fact."

The others smiled, all except for her mother who looked anything but pleased at the innuendo. Linc changed the subject.

"Where are the children, Tanya?" he asked the attractive, tawny-haired woman. "Did you leave them home?"

"Yes. Grandpa and Grandma are babysitting," she answered his question and turned to Joanna to explain, "We have three boys. John is eleven, and a set of four-year-old twins."

"Proud and headstrong—just like their momma," Jake Lassiter declared with a warmly affectionate glance at his wife.

"Like their daddy, you mean," she corrected and arched him a provocative look.

Conscious of Linc's eyes on her, Joanna looked up. There was a mocking gleam in their brown depths. "Only three kids," he murmured. "I guess that proves a ridgerunner doesn't keep his wife barefoot and pregnant all the time." Her pulse skittered under his gaze. "We're a little more civilized than that."

"Don't listen to him, Joanna," Tanya inserted. "Ridgerunners are born cat-wild. You'll never tame one. But you might be able to housebreak him."

Chuckling laughter followed her comment, then the conversation became generalized. When Joanna glanced around to locate Reece and Rachel, her attention was distracted by the view from the sundeck. The blue ridges of the hills seemed to go on forever while the afternoon sun glistened on the lake curling and stretching over the valley.

"Reece was right when he said the view from your house was fantastic," she murmured to Linc.

"You like it, huh?"

"Who wouldn't?" she countered.

"Your mother, maybe," he suggested.

Agreement flickered reluctantly to darken her eyes. Joanna knew her mother wasn't impressed by this view of the countryside. Earlier, she had indicated she had found all the rocks and trees boring.

On the far side of the patio, someone played a few experimental bars of music on a fiddle. Linc turned to look in the direction of the sound.

"Jessie must have arrived," he guessed.

"Who is Jessie?" her mother inquired with an expression of supreme tolerance.

"Jessie Bates lives in a cabin down the road," Joanna explained briefly. She remembered Reece telling her what a good musician Jessie was. "Is he going to play?" she asked Linc.

"With an audience of this size? You bet he

will," he smiled lazily. "Do you want to go over and listen?"

"Yes," Joanna was quick to agree, then hesitated when she glanced at her mother. "Do you want to come?"

"Of course." But the sweet smile of agreement was plainly forced.

With Linc leading the way, they threaded through the gathering crowd until they reached the corner of the sundeck where Jessie was tuning his fiddle. Some of the other guests at the party had brought their instruments as well. Two men had guitars; another had a banjo. There was also a bass and another fiddle.

Joanna was quick to notice, though, that Jessie had dressed for the special occasion. Gone were the baggy overalls. He was wearing a snow-white shirt with a pair of red suspenders holding up his loose pants. With his chin tucked tightly on the violin, he ran the bow over the strings, then stopped to glance over his shoulder at the other musicians.

"How's that sound?" he asked.

The other man with a fiddle shook his head. "Mine has never sounded *that* good." His fellow musicians laughed.

"What ya' need is a set of rattlers to put inside it," Jessie advised his fellow fiddler. "They give it that special tone."

"Rattlers?" he repeated. "What kind of rattlers are you talking about?" The man eyed Jessie with more than a little skepticism. Joanna knew the feeling. Her leg had been pulled many times, too.

"Why, rattlers from a rattlesnake. What else?" Jessie replied with a straight face. "Next time you find a timber rattler out in the woods, stomp on him, an' cut off his rattlers. When you git home, put 'em in your fiddle and it'll sound just like mine."

"Bet it won't," the bass man laughed.

"Are you fellers gonna jaw all day—or are we gonna play something?" Jessie paused to crane his neck, searching the crowd. "Where's the bride and groom-to-be?" Someone pushed Rachel and Reece to the front of the circle. Rachel was blushing a little, but looking very happy. "We're gonna play a song for you," Jessie declared. "Orange blossoms got something to do with weddin's, don't they?" The man with the guitar nodded in answer. "Then, let's play a little *Orange Blossom Special*," Jessie suggested.

Jessie started the song out and the others joined in. Soon, the guests were clapping hands and tapping their feet in time with the music. It seemed to Joanna that the faster the tempo went, the wider the smiles became on everyone's face.

When the song ended, the next selection was more sedate in comparison. Crowded together by the throng of guests, Joanna unconsciously leaned closer to Linc, not wanting to be accidentally separated from him.

"Happy?" His voice murmured the question almost into her ear.

"Mmhum." It was an agreeing sound. She added softly, "I think I'm falling in love with the Ozarks."

"Only with the Ozarks?" Linc challenged quietly.

Her head turned on the pillow of his shoulder so she could look at him. For a second, nothing else existed as their gazes locked. The burst of applause around them signaled the end of the song, and reminded them they weren't alone. His mouth curved in a rueful smile. The bubble of elation didn't go away when Joanna let her attention be drawn back to the small band.

The loud clang of a dinner bell interrupted the country concert before they began another tune. "Time to eat," Linc stated.

Chapter Sixteen

By the time Joanna finished everything on her plate, she was so stuffed she could barely move. All the other guests seemed to be suffering similar conditions—except her mother who had barely taken more than a small spoonful of food from the long buffet table.

Joanna glanced around and noticed her mother sitting with another group, enduring a conversation with one of them. Her fingers gripped the edge of the empty plate balanced on her legs.

Jessie Bates leaned back in his folding chair that faced Joanna and Linc. He rubbed his protruding stomach with his hand. "You did yourself proud on that feast, Linc."

"It was delicious, wasn't it?" Joanna agreed, letting her attention be brought back to their small circle. "I've never been to a barbeque like this before—with a roasted pig and everything. In California, we turn on a transistor radio and charcoal steaks on a grill and call that a barbeque."

"We do it up right in the country," Jessie declared.

"I guess you do," Joanna laughed, but it faded when she saw her mother approaching.

Elizabeth Morgan paused by their chairs to ask, "Have you seen Reece?"

"He's sitting with Rachel by the deck railing." Linc pointed in their direction.

"They make a nice looking couple, don't they?" Jessie remarked.

"How long has he known her?" Elizabeth continued to study the pair seated by themselves.

"Five—six years," Linc replied and her mother looked at him with surprise.

"I hadn't realized that," she admitted on a thoughtful note, and sent a sharp glance at Joanna. "Has he been seeing her all this time?"

"Not exactly," she hedged. "It all happened just recently."

"I think they are being too hasty to marry so soon," Elizabeth stated, letting her opinion be known. "They hardly know each other. I think they should wait. As the old saying goes—marry in haste, repent at leisure."

"Now, we look at it differently in the hills," Jessie disagreed with her. "We think it's a case of—the shorter the wooing, the longer the doing."

"How quaint," her mother murmured with a cloying smile. "If you will excuse me, I think I'll go over and join them."

As she moved gracefully away from their chairs, Jessie watched her with a considering look. "She reminds me of a hen I once had—always jealously guardin' her nest." There was a slight pause before he added, "Only trouble was —she never had no eggs in it."

It was an accurate, yet sad, commentary of her mother's position.

Reece had just left her to take their dirty plates back when Rachel noticed his sister-in-law approaching her. She mentally braced herself for the meeting. She had already made a few guesses about Elizabeth Morgan and had a fair idea of the woman's motives.

"Hello, Mrs. Morgan," she greeted her politely. "Are you enjoying the party?"

"Please call me Elizabeth," she insisted. "After you and Reece are married, it will be terribly confusing if we call each other Mrs. Morgan." As she sat on the redwood bench next to Rachel, she glanced in the direction Reece had taken. "I see Reece has abandoned you already."

Rachel pretended to be unaware of the jibe. "He's taking our plates back."

"Men," Elizabeth murmured in an expressive tone. "They can be so attentive before you're married, then take you for granted afterward, can't they?"

"Sometimes." She didn't disagree. Her gaze followed Reece as he paused to speak to an attractive young woman.

"You'll get used to that eventually," Elizabeth murmured. "The Morgan men have always been known for their roving eye." She smiled at Rachel, as if they shared a common experience. "Of course, they are experts at sweeping women off their feet. I should know. I was married to one."

"You were married to Reece's brother, weren't you?" Rachel pretended to recall the face, fully aware Elizabeth's interest wasn't directed at her late husband.

"His younger brother, yes," she nodded. "He was a great deal like Reece—in looks and temperament." She studied Rachel for a long second. "I must say that I admire you."

"Oh?" She found that difficult to believe.

"Yes. There aren't many women who would tackle a new husband and plunge into a new lifestyle all in one leap—without even testing the water," Elizabeth explained her compliment —a backhanded one.

"I suppose not." It was going to be a big adjustment.

"I do hope you'll like living in California. It will take some getting used to, I'm sure," Elizabeth remarked with feigned sympathy. "I don't suppose you've had much experience dealing with a housekeeping staff. Reece has a beautiful home, very luxurious." She was not too subtly pointing out their background differences. "Of course, he has to. His business requires him to do so much entertaining—formal parties— things like that."

"Of course," Rachel murmured.

"If you would ever need any help, I hope you'll call on me." She assumed an air of false modesty. "I've given thousands of dinner parties so— arranging all the fine details is practically second nature to me."

"Thank you. It's kind of you to offer." She'd call the devil's wife before she'd ask Elizabeth.

"We're practically family," Elizabeth reminded her. "Reece and I have always been very close." But not as close as Elizabeth had wanted them to be, Rachel guessed. She was being studied with a critical eye. "And clothes. I'll take you to some of my favorite shops where we can buy you a whole new wardrobe so you won't be embarrassed when you're with the other wives."

The comment had struck a vulnerable nerve, making Rachel very self-conscious of the polka-dot dress she'd made herself. She glanced at it, silently comparing it with the elegant outfit Elizabeth was wearing.

"I hadn't thought about that." Probably none of her clothes were suitable for her new lifestyle in California.

"I doubt if Reece has given you a chance to think about anything," Elizabeth declared. "I need to have a talk with him. Marriage is difficult under the best of circumstances. I'd hate to see the two of you start out on the wrong foot."

"Yes." It was just a reply, meaning nothing.

"I'm so glad we've had this chance to chat." Elizabeth pressed her hand on top of Rachel's in a falsely affectionate gesture. "I'd like to think that we'll be friends."

"Yes, it would be nice." Even if she doubted it could ever happen.

"I'm monopolizing your time and I didn't intend to do that." She had cast a few doubts in Rachel's mind. Her mission was accomplished. "You have a lot of friends here and I'm sure you want to spend some time with them. Since you and Reece are getting married so soon, it might be your last opportunity to do so before you're uprooted." She planted one last seed before departing with a self-satisfied gleam in her eye.

As Reece attempted to tactfully excuse himself from the company of a native Californian who had recently migrated to the Ozark hills, his glance strayed to the railing where he'd left Rachel. He stiffened when he saw Elizabeth sitting with her, his jaw hardening into a grim line.

"Excuse me." He abruptly took his leave of the man without waiting for a polite opening.

Elizabeth was already walking away as he crossed the deck to rejoin Rachel. She had turned away to view the panorama of the hills, but not before Reece had noticed the troubled look in her thoughtful expression. He had known the minute Elizabeth had arrived that she would try to make some kind of trouble. After all he'd gone through, he wasn't going to lose Rachel now.

He came up beside her. "That's a long face to be wearing at your engagement party," he remarked with deliberate lightness.

Rachel turned to smile at him. "I was thinking."

"About what?" Reece prompted.

"Us."

"What about us?" He gently prodded the information from her.

"I was just wondering whether we are doing the right thing—getting married so quickly and all," she admitted with a certain hesitation, aware he had no doubts.

"Elizabeth had something to do with your second thoughts, didn't she?" Reece was certain of the source.

"Indirectly," Rachel avoided putting all the blame on his sister-in-law. "Our lives have been so different, Reece. What do I know about dinner parties and entertaining important clients? Maybe I won't fit in."

"You will."

She shook her head, disagreeing. "I'm not at all like Elizabeth."

His smile was amused. "Thank God."

"Please," she protested his attempt to make

light of the situation. "I'm trying to discuss this with you."

"After you have already discussed it with Elizabeth," he replied with vague impatience. "Why did you listen to her, Rachel? Don't you realize she is jealous?"

"I'm not blind, Reece. I know she's in love with you." Rachel recognized the signs. "But that doesn't mean the points she raised are not valid. They are. Maybe we shouldn't rush into this."

"There is only one valid reason that matters," he insisted. "I love you, Rachel, and I want you for my wife. Anything else Elizabeth may have said means nothing. Yes, there will be many adjustments to make," Reece conceded. "But we'll make them together. *Together*, Rachel. Do you understand?"

"Yes." Nothing seemed impossible with the strength of their love on their side.

Bending his head, Reece kissed her lightly, but warmly. "Wait here while I find Elizabeth," he requested. "It's time I had a little talk with her."

"Don't do that," Rachel protested, not wanting to make trouble.

"I must," Reece insisted. "She has to understand that I won't allow her to come between us." His hand caressed her cheek. "I know what I'm doing, Rachel. If I don't end this now, she will keep trying. And I won't take the risk that next time she might succeed."

Rachel couldn't argue against the wisdom of his decision. She guessed that he knew his sister-in-law much better than she did. When he walked away, she didn't attempt to stop him.

It was several minutes before Reece finally located Elizabeth in the party crowd. She was with Linc and Joanna, looking faintly bored. When she saw him walking toward her, she brightened visibly. Reece wasn't taken in by that artificial charm.

"I'd like a word with you, Elizabeth," he stated, taking her arm to lead her away after nodding briefly to Linc. He ignored Joanna's curious glance, not wanting to involve his niece in this dispute.

When they were off by themselves, Elizabeth viewed his hard expression with an innocent look. "Is something wrong?"

"I knew when you arrived this morning, you would try to make trouble," he stated.

"Trouble?" She blinked. "I don't know what you mean."

"You have been trying to convince Rachel that we should postpone the wedding," Reece accused smoothly.

"Now, that is nonsense. I did nothing of the kind," Elizabeth denied his charge. "We discussed living in California and I offered to help in any way I could to—"

Reece wasn't interested in her version of the conversation. "It doesn't matter what you discussed. Rachel and I are getting married next week—as planned," he emphasized. "There is nothing you can say or do to change that."

"I wouldn't *presume* to try," she replied with wounded dignity.

"You would *presume* a great deal if you thought you could succeed."

"How can you say that when I was only trying to be helpful?" she protested.

"We don't need your kind of help. Not now—and not later."

"Well, if that's the way you feel about it—" Elizabeth began with an exaggerated air of pride.

"I'll tell you exactly the way I feel about it." Reece cut through the niceties. "You weren't invited here. Of course, that's never stopped you. You barge in whether you're welcome or not. If it wasn't for Joanna, I would have told you to get lost a long time ago. But she is my brother's daughter, so I have tolerated you. But no more." He was hardened against the pallor that spread over her face. "Make whatever excuse you wish but take the next plane back to L.A. Is that clear?" he challenged.

Elizabeth held herself stiffly, proudly fighting back tears. "Very."

"Good," he stated. "I will tell Rachel you're leaving. There will be no need for you to speak to her again."

An exchange of goodbyes would have been hypocritical at this point. Without saying another word, Reece turned on his heel and walked away. Elizabeth stood rigidly, staring after him.

When Joanna noticed her mother slowly returning, her gaze sharpened. Although her mother was trying to appear calm and composed, Joanna observed the fine tension that put a strain in her expression and the pallor beneath her rouged complexion.

"Is something wrong, Mother?" she asked the instant she joined them.

"It's this sun," Elizabeth replied tightly. "It's given me a terrible headache. Would you mind very much if we left the party? All this heat and noise is just making it worse."

Joanna hesitated, then glanced at Linc. "Could you drive us back to the cabin?"

"Of course," he agreed, making his own assessment of her mother.

The party was regaining its former level of gaiety. Hardly anyone noticed them leave as they walked around the house to Linc's car. In the passenger seat, her mother reclined against the headrest and closed her eyes. Her attitude silenced any conversation that might have been made during the short drive to the cabin.

They entered the log home by the front door, which had been left unlocked. "Why don't you sit on the sofa, Mother?" Joanna suggested. "I'll get you some aspirin and a glass of water."

"Thank you." It was a very subdued Elizabeth who sat on the cushioned sofa.

"I'll get them for you, Joanna," Linc volunteered. "You make your mother comfortable."

"Okay." She was grateful for his offer, but at

the moment she was too concerned about her mother to express it.

Picking up a decorative pillow, Joanna plumped it to put behind her mother's head. The offer was waved aside with an autocratic hand.

"Would you telephone the airline for me?" her mother requested.

"The airline?" Joanna stared, then realized her mother was probably intending to book return passage. "We can do that later. Just sit back and rest—"

"Stop fussing over me," she protested when Joanna attempted again to put the pillow behind her head. "I don't have a headache. I only used that as an excuse to leave the party." Joanna straightened, irritated at the way she had been fooled. "Call the airline," her mother ordered. "I want to make reservations on the first flight back to Los Angeles."

"Mother, you just got here," Joanna argued the necessity for doing it this minute.

"And Reece has ordered me to leave," Elizabeth replied. She didn't have to fake the hurt look that wavered in her eyes.

"I can't believe that," Joanna frowned in stunned doubt. "Why would he do such a thing?"

Her chin quivered. "He doesn't want me here. He thinks I'm trying to come between him and Rachel. All I did was offer to help and he accused me of interfering."

"Were you, Mother?" She wouldn't put it past her.

"No," she denied it. "I think Reece is making

a foolish mistake by marrying that woman. They have absolutely nothing in common. But I *was* making an effort to be nice. And he repays me by practically throwing me out. After all the years I've—"

The sentence was left unfinished as Linc returned to the living room, carrying a glass of water and an aspirin bottle. He brought it to the sofa.

"Here you are, Mrs. Morgan." He handed them to her.

"Thank you," she murmured.

Linc waited until she had taken them, then glanced at Joanna. "We'd better be getting back to the party."

Hesitating, Joanna glanced at her mother. She didn't know what was going on, or how much of her mother's story was truth. She couldn't have completely fabricated such a tale.

"You go ahead without me," Joanna advised him reluctantly. "I'm going to stay with Mother a little while."

"Is it necessary?" he frowned in sharp question.

"Something's come up." Joanna couldn't tell him about it, not yet. "I can't explain."

"All right." But it was a grudging acceptance of her decision. "I'll see you later."

Her teeth bit at the inside of her lip. Joanna knew he didn't understand why her mother needed her. She could read it in the impatient stride that carried him to the front door.

"There have been times in the past, Joanna,"

her mother sighed when the door had closed behind Linc, "when we haven't always agreed with each other but I'm so glad you're here with me. I've never felt so abandoned."

It was the assurance Joanna needed to convince her she had made the right choice. She sat down on the sofa next to her mother.

"I still don't understand why Reece would do such a thing," Joanna stated her confusion.

"Neither do I," she admitted with a bewildered shake of her artfully bleached hair.

"But he must have given some other explanation," Joanna persisted in her search for the rest of the story.

"Reece claimed he . . . he only tolerated me because of you." She lifted her tear-bright eyes to gaze at Joanna. "That hurt."

She had never witnessed this display of vulnerability in her mother before. It touched her, moving her to a deep sympathy.

"Momma, I'm sorry," she whispered.

"You will fly home with me, won't you?" Elizabeth reached out to tightly grasp her daughter's hand in an earnest appeal.

"Do you mean today? Now?" Joanna was startled, reluctant.

"Reece said he didn't want me here," she reminded. "I have to leave now."

"But—" Her troubled brown eyes glanced toward the front door that Linc had went out a few minutes ago.

"How can you hesitate?" There was a kind of desperation in her mother's question.

Her shoulders drooped in resignation. "I'll go with you," Joanna agreed. "But I have to call Linc and let him know."

"Linc?" She took her hand away from Joanna's. "Why should you tell him anything?"

"He's expecting to see me again and I—" She tried to explain.

There was a mixture of pain and scorn in her mother's expression. "Reece has his 'Daisy Mae.' Don't tell me you think you've found your Lil' Abner?" The acid sting was back in her mother's voice, if not at full strength. Joanna darted her an angry look. "Oh, I grant you he's a handsome man, if you go for the earthy type. But, Joanna, you barely know him." Elizabeth tempered her criticism of Linc.

"That doesn't change the way I feel," she insisted.

"No doubt you are attracted to him," her mother conceded. "But, love? In a month, you'll forget what he looks like. That's the way it always happens with these holiday romances."

It wasn't a holiday romance but there was nothing to be gained by arguing that point with her mother. She kept silent as her mother stood up.

"We haven't much time," Elizabeth prodded at her. "You'd better go upstairs and start packing. I'll call the airline." When Joanna continued to remain seated, impatience raced through Elizabeth's expression. "If you feel you have to call this . . . Linc Wilder, you can do it from the airport."

* * *

With the car turned into the rental agency, Joanna slipped the receipt in her purse and hurried into the main lobby of the airport terminal. Her mother stood impatiently beside a display case.

"I have the tickets." She handed Joanna hers. "They'll be boarding the plane in a few minutes."

"You go ahead to the gate," Joanna urged. "I'll be there in a minute."

"Where are you going?" Elizabeth frowned.

"To call Linc." She was already backing away in the direction of the phone booths. "It won't take long."

"Be quick about it."

The more she tried to hurry, the longer it seemed to take. Joanna rummaged through her purse for the change for the pay telephone, then waited impatiently while the phone rang. The housekeeper answered, and she had to wait again while the woman went to fetch Linc from the party. She almost sighed in relief when she heard his voice on the other end of the line.

"Linc. It's Joanna," she identified herself quickly.

"Hello." Warmth was injected into his second greeting. "Are you ready to come back to the party? I'll come pick you up."

"No. That is—" She was interrupted by the announcement of an arriving flight over the airport's public address system.

"Where are you?" Linc questioned.

"At the airport."

"The airport? What are you doing there?" There was sharp confusion in his voice.

"Mother's flying back to California"—Joanna paused and closed her eyes—"and I'm going with her."

"What?" It was a stunned reply. "Why?"

"Mother and Reece had a falling out and—" She didn't have time to explain. "It's a long story, Linc, and I don't have time to go into it." She waited for him to say something, but there was only silence. "I just wanted to call and tell you goodbye before I left," she added lamely.

"That's it, huh?" Linc challenged. "Just goodbye and it's been nice knowing you?"

"No." She was half-angry. "Try to understand, Linc. Under the circumstances, I can't stay."

"I understand all right," he replied. "The message is loud and clear. You go ahead and enjoy your champagne flight back to L.A. I have guests and a barbeque waiting for me."

Joanna knew what he was saying but she refused to acknowledge it. "If that's the way you feel—" she began indignantly.

"What do you expect me to say?" he cut in angrily. "You said it all, Joanna, when you said goodbye."

The line went dead. Her fingers tightened on the receiver as she realized Linc had hung up on her. He hadn't even tried to understand her situation.

Slowly, she returned the receiver to its hook

and gathered up her purse and tickets. Tears were spilling down her lashes. Joanna wiped them away as she walked to the gate area.

The flight was already boarding when Joanna arrived at the gate where her mother was waiting for her. "Did you talk to Reece?" Elizabeth asked before Joanna could say anything.

"Reece? No, I didn't." She shook her head, numbed by the pain inside.

Disappointment clouded her mother's face. "I thought . . . He might have . . ." There was a dispirited shake of her head. "It doesn't matter. We'd better go. They've already begun boarding."

The party was still going strong at the Wilder ranch but Linc had isolated himself from it. He stood alone at the deck railing. His gaze wasn't admiring the view of the lake and hills. It was fastened to the western sky. A half-empty drink was in his hand. He didn't hear Reece and Rachel walk up to him.

"Where's Joanna?" Reece inquired with curious concern.

It was the use of her name that penetrated Linc's mind. He turned to look blankly at his friend for an instant. Then his gaze lowered to the drink he was holding.

"She's gone." His voice was flat—unemotional. "She called a little while ago to say she was flying back to California with her mother." Linc downed a swallow of watered-down whiskey, unaware of the glance Rachel and Reece exchanged. "Do you remember the talk we had awhile back, Reece—about all the responsibility that was suddenly mine after my dad died?"

"Yes." Reece frowned, unsure what that had to do with his niece.

"All that's over with now," he declared and exhaled a long breath. "Mom is with Dad, Sharon's married, and David is out on his own." His gaze swept the ranchland. "This place practically runs by itself now. I don't have anyone to worry about except myself." He looked at the glass again and shook his head. A wry slant of amusement lifted a corner of his mouth when Linc raised his glance to Reece. "I was wild as a young'un." There was something absent, almost brooding that claimed his features. "It's been a long time since I've been on a good drunk."

Chapter Seventeen

$\mathcal{A}$ ll the furniture in the log home was covered with sheets, giving the place a ghostly air. Linc paused in the middle of the living room and glanced around. His features were drawn unnaturally taut, because for him, it was haunted with Joanna's ghost.

"Is that you in thare, Linc?" Jessie Bates pressed his face to the wire mesh of the screen door, cupping his hands around his eyes to peer inside.

"Yeah, it's me." The reply was rough and unfriendly, showing the edges of a short temper.

Jessie didn't wait on an invitation, just opened the screen door and came in. "I heard the truck go by my place. I didn't know whether it was you or somebody snoopin' around so I thought I'd better check." He glanced around the house. "Is everything all right here?"

"Yeah," Linc nodded curtly. "I promised Reece I'd check to see that it was all locked up."

"I guess the newlyweds got off to Californy okay," Jessie surmised.

"Yep."

Jessie peered at him closely, partially lowering one eyelid. "You still grumpin' over Joanna, ain't cha?"

"Why don't you mind your own damned business, Jessie?" Linc snapped, not liking the personal observation. He stalked toward the door, not wanting to hear any more of Jessie's comments.

"I always figured you to be the kind of a man to take the bull by the horns." Jessie followed him, baggy overalls and all.

"Is that a fact?" His reply was abrupt and loaded with sarcasm. Once outside, Linc waited until Jessie was on the stoop, then locked the door.

"I never guessed you'd turn out to be one of those tame fellas that let's a gal tell ya' how things is gonna be," Jessie didn't let up. "You want her, don't ya?"

"Lay off, Jessie." It was a tautly issued order.

"You jest don't understand women." The Ozark character shook his head. "When they say 'no,' they mean 'yes.' And when they wanta stay, they go," he explained, then paused to suggest, "If'n I was you, I'd go bring her back."

Linc stared at him, irritated and tense, but he said nothing in reply.

The living room of the Morgans' California home was a cool green and white, furnished with an understated elegance. Looking very radiant and proud, Rachel sat on the armrest of a jade-green chair where Reece was sitting. Her arm was around his shoulder in a natural display of affection while his was curved around her waist in light possession.

A wistful quality crept into Joanna's smile as she looked at the couple. "Marriage certainly agrees with you two," she said the obvious. "I don't even need to ask if you're happy."

"Ecstatic," Rachel declared. "I have you to thank for that, Joanna. If you hadn't shamed me into that dinner invitation, I probably would still be running from him."

"Sooner or later, I would have caught you," Reece stated.

"He was running out of patience," Joanna remembered from her seat on the edge of the ivory couch.

"I wish you had been able to fly back for the wedding." There was regret in Rachel's glance. "I understand why you couldn't, but—"

"I'd like to have been there," she admitted, and paused to mentally brace herself to speak his name. "Linc was best man, wasn't he?" She tried to sound happy and uncaring, interested only by the aspect of their wedding party.

"Yes, he was." Reece wasn't fooled.

Joanna tried to fake an idle curiosity. "How is Linc?"

"Fine," he nodded and closely watched his niece.

The doorbell rang, and Rachel slipped off the arm of the chair. "I'll answer it." She laid a hand on his shoulder to keep Reece in his seat, then walked toward the foyer off the living room.

It was a natural gesture of belonging that Joanna couldn't help noticing. "Rachel is already regarding this as her home, isn't she?" she remarked to her uncle.

"It is her home . . . *our* home," he corrected himself with a smile. Then he casually brought the subject back to Linc. "I was under the impression that you were becoming serious about Linc before you left."

She lowered her gaze, agitated by the direct comment. "I'd rather not discuss it." Immediately Joanna contradicted herself by saying, "Linc didn't give me a chance to explain why I had to leave."

There were muffled voices in the foyer as Rachel greeted the caller at the door. Joanna paid no attention to them. Her back was to the entry area, so she didn't see the tall, dark-haired man pause at the living room opening.

"I never guessed Elizabeth would insist that you leave with her," Reece stated. "It's ultimately my fault you had to leave at all." His startled gaze noticed Linc Wilder standing there. He started to say something to Joanna, but Linc motioned him to keep quiet.

"Linc should have listened," Joanna insisted. "I don't blame you, Reece. There are times when *I'd* like to slap Mother's face. But . . . with all her faults, she's still my mother. What kind of daughter would I have been if I hadn't stood beside her?"

"I know," Reece murmured.

"Linc should have understood that," Joanna rephrased her earlier statement, with a little more anger in her voice this time. "He's impossible, Reece. I mean, there he was telling *me* that I was telling *him* goodbye! And I was doing nothing of the kind!"

"Why didn't you tell me to shut up and listen?" Linc asked quietly.

His voice quivered through her, shocking her into stillness. For a split second, Joanna thought she was losing her mind. She half-turned to look behind her. Her heart stopped beating when she saw Linc standing there.

Her gaze ran in disbelief over his well-muscled, long-bodied frame. His face seemed leaner, the rugged planes of his features more pronounced. Joanna was conscious that Linc was looking her over, too, almost devouring her wth his eyes. That did nothing to calm the erratic behavior of her pulse.

"What are you doing here, Linc?" Joanna stood up slowly to face him, afraid she might be guessing wrong about his reason.

She was only partially aware of Rachel and Reece slipping quietly out of the room to leave her alone with Linc. When he walked forward to enter the room, Joanna noticed the bottle of champagne in his hand.

"Why does any man leave the hills?" Linc countered her question with one of his own, then supplied the answer. "To find himself a woman."

Linc didn't stop until he was squarely in front of her. His earthy virility reached out, disturbing her senses. It would have been easy to take the last step into his arms, but Joanna waited, breathlessly, unable to speak.

"In my case," Linc went on, "I had to fly half way across the country to find the right one." The dark glow of gold fire was in his eyes when he looked at her, searching her expression. When he spoke again, his voice was husky with intense longing. "It's lonely back there without you, Joanna."

Her breath caught in her throat. For an instant, she wasn't able to reply. "I've been lonely here, too," she admitted.

He appeared to lean toward her, as if to sweep her into his arms, then stopped. "There's one way to end our misery."

Inside, she was straining toward him, but some invisible force held her in check, too. "What's that?" Joanna whispered.

"Marry me," Linc said simply.

A smile began to curve its line along her lips. "I'll marry you," she accepted and added her own conditions to the proposal. "But—only if you promise to keep me barefoot and pregnant."

His arms were around her and it was the only

place in the world she wanted to be. Joanna closed her eyes, loving him more than she had ever believed it was possible to love a man.

His mouth came down to bruise her lips in a hungry kiss, but Joanna had been without the particular satisfaction only he could give just as long as he had. This was a feasting time. Both of them were trembling long before they had their fill.

His heart was beating so loudly, Joanna could hear it above the drumming of her own. She leaned weakly against the wide wall of his chest, momentarily satisfied just to be in his arms.

"I guess I didn't need this after all," Linc stated thickly.

One arm was withdrawn from around her. Its loss, as much as his cryptic statement, prompted Joanna to glance around. The champagne bottle was still in his hand. She had been so absorbed in loving him, she hadn't been conscious of the bottle's alien shape against her body.

It took her a second to understand why Linc had brought the champagne. It was so obvious when she realized it. He had believed she preferred champagne dinners to barbeques. The gesture of bringing champagne proved the lengths he would go to have her.

"If you had bothered to ask me," Joanna murmured, "I would have told you that I don't like champagne."

"There are times when you can be as stubborn

as a Missouri mule, Joanna," Linc declared on a vibrantly possessive note. "But I have the feeling I'll make a ridgerunner's wife out of you yet."

She partially withdrew from his embrace, but continued to rely on his steadying support as she bent to slip off her heels.

"What are you doing?" he frowned despite the hint of amusement in his voice.

"A proper ridgerunner's wife is supposed to be barefoot," Joanna reminded him. "I can handle that part of it, but I'll need your participation for the rest of it."

He laughed and pulled her back into his arms. "I'll handle it—in my own good time," Linc promised, tossing the champagne bottle onto the couch cushions. "I'm not sure that I fancy the idea of your momma marching me down the aisle with a shotgun at my back."

The reference to her mother sobered Joanna, reminding her of the reason for the separation. "You do understand why I had to come back with her, don't you?" she asked.

"Now, I do," Linc assured her. "At the time you left, I didn't. I thought she had influenced you into changing your mind about me." A wry smile crooked his mouth, a very handsome mouth. "It would be safe to say that I'm not your mother's first choice as a son-in-law."

"But I'm not marrying you so she can have a son." Joanna would have liked her mother's approval, but it wouldn't change anything if she didn't have it. In all fairness to her mother, she had to say, "She has changed a little—since that incident with Reece. When our first baby is born, I wouldn't be surprised if she came to the hills to see it."

"Let's do some practicing first before we get down to the serious business of making a baby," Linc suggested.

"Anytime," Joanna murmured provocatively.

If you enjoyed
this book...

...you will enjoy a Special Edition Book Club membership even more.

It will bring you each new title, as soon as it is published every month, delivered right to your door.

15-Day Free Trial Offer

We will send you 6 new Silhouette Special Editions to keep for 15 days absolutely free! If you decide not to keep them, send them back to us, you pay nothing. But if you enjoy them as much as we think you will, keep them and pay the invoice enclosed with your trial shipment. You will then automatically become a member of the Special Edition Book Club and receive 6 more romances every month. There is no minimum number of books to buy and you can cancel at any time.

Silhouette Special Edition

Coming Next Month

Magnolia Moon by Sondra Stanford

Nicole went to New Orleans to look for a job.
Instead, she found magic at the Mardi Gras. Ryan
St. James was a man with everything under
control—until he met Nicole. She made his blood
run like a river after the storm. He made her
breath race like wind through the trees. Together
they challenged the very stars and wrote their love
across the Southern sky.

Web Of Passion by Nancy John

The feelings Dirk Lancaster, outback lord, raised
in Risa were enough to leave her aching for his
every touch. In this land of torrential rains and dry
spells of searing intensity, Risa could blossom into
a woman open to life, ready for love, and ripe for
the one man who could tame her heart and
master the raging sun.

Autumn Harvest by Angel Milan

Botanist Tara Deer had plenty of plans. Then she
met Kane Boland and the dreams she had once
nurtured grew to include the lean Oklahoma
rancher who held her heart and happiness in his
hands. He could touch her with passion, then
bring her to a peak of ecstasy and leave her
trembling with desire. Without this man,
all her dreams were but empty air.

Silhouette Special Edition

Coming Next Month

Heartstorm by Jane Converse

Cocos Island was a land of mystery, of steaming
jungles, barren rocks and pagan majesty, a land of
romance with a link to the past. Here Terry Long
and Dean Saunders met and clashed and came
together in stormy passion beneath a canopy of
trees and a golden island sun. Here they fought
their way through their own misconceptions
and misjudgments to greet tomorrow's dawn.

Collision Course by Carole Halston

At last the girl who had never lacked for anything
had everything she wanted. Lindy Randolph met
her match when she met Neil Hammonds. He was
a man to dream about; the challenge was to make
him dream of her. Lindy's breath caught and her
heart quickened when he was near and she
longed to rise with him to the heights
that passion promised.

Proud Vintage by Brenna Drummond

Hurt by love, Katherine Carson was afraid to trust
any man. Then, in California's Napa Valley, she
met Adam Redmont, a man of pride, power and
passion. Adam taught her to trust again, to express
herself with a touch, a look. Together they lit a fire
even time could not put out and shared the
secrets that only lovers know.

Silhouette Special Edition

MORE ROMANCE FOR
A SPECIAL WAY TO RELAX

$1.95 each

1 ☐ TERMS OF SURRENDER Dailey
2 ☐ INTIMATE STRANGERS Hastings
3 ☐ MEXICAN RHAPSODY Dixon
4 ☐ VALAQUEZ BRIDE Vitek
5 ☐ PARADISE POSTPONED Converse
6 ☐ SEARCH FOR A NEW DAWN Douglass
7 ☐ SILVER MIST Stanford
8 ☐ KEYS TO DANIEL'S HOUSE Halston
9 ☐ ALL OUR TOMORROWS Baxter
10 ☐ TEXAS ROSE Thiels
11 ☐ LOVE IS SURRENDER Thornton
12 ☐ NEVER GIVE YOUR HEART Sinclair
13 ☐ BITTER VICTORY Beckman
14 ☐ EYE OF THE HURRICANE Keene
15 ☐ DANGEROUS MAGIC James
16 ☐ MAYAN MOON Carr
17 ☐ SO MANY TOMORROWS John
18 ☐ A WOMAN'S PLACE Hamilton

19 ☐ DECEMBER'S WINE Shaw
20 ☐ NORTHERN LIGHTS Musgrave
21 ☐ ROUGH DIAMOND Hastings
22 ☐ ALL THAT GLITTERS Howard
23 ☐ LOVE'S GOLDEN SHADOW Charles
24 ☐ GAMBLE OF DESIRE Dixon
25 ☐ TEARS AND RED ROSES Hardy
26 ☐ A FLIGHT OF SWALLOWS Scott
27 ☐ A MAN WITH DOUBTS Wisdom
28 ☐ THE FLAMING TREE Ripy
29 ☐ YEARNING OF ANGELS Bergen
30 ☐ BRIDE IN BARBADOS Stephens
31 ☐ TEARS OF YESTERDAY Baxter
32 ☐ A TIME TO LOVE Douglass
33 ☐ HEATHER'S SONG Palmer
34 ☐ MIXED BLESSING Sinclair
35 ☐ STORMY CHALLENGE James
36 ☐ FOXFIRE LIGHT Dailey

SILHOUETTE SPECIAL EDITION, Department SE/2
1230 Avenue of the Americas
New York, NY 10020

Please send me the books I have checked above. I am enclosing $_____
(please add 50¢ to cover postage and handling. NYS and NYC residents
please add appropriate sales tax). Send check or money order—no cash or
C.O.D.'s please. Allow six weeks for delivery.

NAME _____

ADDRESS _____

CITY _____ STATE/ZIP _____

Silhouette Desire
15-Day Trial Offer

A new romance series
that explores
contemporary relationships
in exciting detail

Four Silhouette Desire romances, free for 15 days!
We'll send you four new Silhouette Desire romances
to look over for 15 days, absolutely free! If you decide
not to keep the books, return them and owe nothing.

Four books a month, free home delivery. If you like
Silhouette Desire romances as much as we think you
will, keep them and return your payment with the
invoice. Then we will send you four new books every
month to preview, just as soon as they are published.
You pay only for the books you decide to keep, and
you never pay postage and handling.

READERS' COMMENTS ON SILHOUETTE SPECIAL EDITIONS:

"I just finished reading the first six Silhouette Special Edition Books and I had to take the opportunity to write you and tell you how much I enjoyed them. I enjoyed all the authors in this series. Best wishes on your Silhouette Special Editions line and many thanks."

—B.H.*, Jackson, OH

"The Special Editions are really special and I enjoyed them very much! I am looking forward to next month's books."

—R.M.W.*, Melbourne, FL

"I've just finished reading four of your first six Special Editions and I enjoyed them very much. I like the more sensual detail and longer stories. I will look forward each month to your new Special Editions."

—L.S.*, Visalia, CA

"Silhouette Special Editions are — 1.) Superb! 2.) Great! 3.) Delicious! 4.) Fantastic! . . . Did I leave anything out? These are books that an adult woman can read . . . I love them!"

—H.C.*, Monterey Park, CA

* names available on request